I Still Think about You

Arpit Vageria

Srishti
PUBLISHERS & DISTRIBUTORS

Srishti Publishers & Distributors
Registered Office: N-16, C.R. Park
New Delhi – 110 019
Corporate Office: 212A, Peacock Lane
Shahpur Jat, New Delhi – 110 049
editorial@srishtipublishers.com

First published by
Srishti Publishers & Distributors in 2016

10 9 8 7 6 5 4 3 2 1

Printed and bound in India

Acknowledgements

I will begin by thanking my grandfather, Mr. Sohan Lal Vageria for his unconditional love and blessings; my parents, Mr. Dilip Vageria and Mrs. Vandana Vageria for being the loveliest couple and also for their undying support and encouragement; my elder brother, Ankit Vageria, for always being there whenever I am in trouble and for being my 2 a.m. buddy; my sister-in-law, Donika Vageria for her unwavering faith in me; and to the world's cutest kid ever, my niece, Maahi Vageria for looking vanilla-ice-cream-scoop cute and for making my life with her smile. I can go on and on talking about her and she'll be more than proud to read when she grows up to be a beautiful young woman someday. There's so much to thank my entire family for, but I thank them for being able to understand my profession and commitments that come along with it.

No thank you is big enough for Swapnil Kothari sir, for he not only constantly motivated me but also guided me by taking away the sting from his words intelligently, and for being with me through every phase of my life and guiding me on what's right and what's not, both personally and professionally. Even if I become 1% of what he is, my life will be made and I'll have no regrets from this world. I have never ever in my life met as humble a person as him and as amazing a thinker that he is.

A big thank you is due to 'Renaissance' and 'Indore Indira College' families for always loving me.

Some of the names without whom I consider my life incomplete and bland are Aditi Solanki, for being the first ever person to praise my writing by making me believe that I can write and that people will read and like it; Riddhi, for being the most amazing human being ever; Vankush for always believing in me and my potential; and Novoneel, for being there with me in all the ups and downs of life and supporting me in the best possible way. Rohit Raikwar, Ankit, Piyush Shah and Romil Jain for being the best ever flat-mates and giving me so many memories to cherish.

I am grateful to Shashi ma'am, Kuldeep, Zeba, Shikha, Manali, Amruta, Pratiksha, Pooja, Nageen and Apoorv for always being a wonderful company.

I would also like to thank some of my childhood friends – Rohan Raikwar, Manoj Punjabi, Himanshu Jain, Vinay Sachdeva, Pramod Jaiswal, Prateek Vyas, Ulhas Baviskar, and Deep Bhand for making my world better and interesting.

Heartfelt thanks to some friends who kept me grounded and taught me to see life from a fresh perspective – Pooja Anjania, Vinay Anjania, Saurabh sir, Naveen, Sachi, Preeti Singh ma'am, Ayush, Manisha, Ayushi, Saloni, Supriti, Mayank, Sumit, Gaurav, Shubham, Kunal, Kroni, Sukriti, Mithun and Karan.

I would now like to thank my publisher for accepting my story and showing huge interest in the same. Thanks for being ever so supportive, team Srishti Publishers.

And lastly, to myself, for being able to complete this wonderful book.

January 2005

Aamir was sweating in the cold because he was scared. He hadn't spoken much, and Dhruv didn't press him for it too. His shirt was soaked in several places when Dhruv took him to a paragliding destination close to Rohtang Pass. Looking at the people swinging, dancing and shouting in the air made Dhruv think, 'I'd like to try it too, at least for once in my life.' And that's how he decided to take his first paragliding flight over the mountains along with Aamir, though much against Aamir's wish.

'I am just not doing it, and I will not allow you to do it either, Dhruv,' Aamir said.

'Of course we're doing it. Imagine this unforgettable thrill that we'll remember for a lifetime, Aamir. You just can't afford to say no to this.'

'I'm not that brave, Dhruv; nor am I that crazy. I just can't do this. Please let it go. Got it?'

'That's great. I'm not that brave either. We'll face the fear and the adventure together. This is going to be awesome, bro!' Dhruv was literally shouting at the top of his voice.

'Did you hear what that pilot said? You can't sit before you take off, else you'll roll down the mountains and we're not responsible for that.' Aamir looked hysterical.

'That's a part of his job: to explain the procedure. The take off will be much easier than what you think it will be. You need to take just a few steps running down the hill and you'll be in the air. Don't you want to get the closest feeling of being a bird? It's a fun, even safe way to experience flight in its simplest form,' Dhruv tried to pacify him.

'Dhruv, please try and understand. I am near to pissing in my pants after seeing them shout and hang in the middle of nowhere. Alright, everything turns out fine usually. But what if we are those unusual, unlucky ones who don't make it? No, Dhruv! Never ever am I doing this. It's too much of a risk. Don't be stupid.'

'And I can't afford to miss out on this fun. Even if you're not coming, I am going to do this, all by myself. I am going to jump if you're not doing it. See me dead or alive...your choice, Aamir.'

'You can't make puppy eyes to get your way on this matter of life and death, Dhruv.'

'I am not looking back, Aamir.' He said, as he drew close to the paragliding pilot and paid him for a ride.

'Make it for two.'

'What?'

'That's what you heard, you dog; you aren't really leaving me with an option here. I am just doing it for you, to see you happy and nothing else.'

Dhruv ran to hug Aamir. They smiled, laughed and got ready for an experience like never before. Both of them were quite unsettled though.

'Are you ready for this?' the pilot asked. They both gave their bravest smiles.

After a short test run, they were both attached with two separate paragliding pilots and they didn't look back when their instructor asked them to run.

They began to fly. They were settled comfortably in the harness and experienced the indescribable freedom of flight and fright. Once in the air, the pilot was able to maintain and gain altitude using rising air currents and thermals. They continued to fly over the mountains, driven by the winds, admiring the landscape, enjoying the silence. They touched the tress beneath them with their feet, and with every rise in height, the view became incredible; the world below grew smaller and smaller All their problems, fears and anxieties started disappearing, and their minds were set free like birds set free from their cages.

After a wonderful flight, when they were preparing to land, the pilot explained that they just had to run down once to the earth. He simply steered it into the landing area, and glided down for a very gentle touchdown on earth. As they touched the ground with a thrust, Aamir and Dhruv laughed out loud looking at each other, overjoyed at having fulfilled their dream of flying.

'We made it. We're alive. We are the superheroes…' Aamir was shouting all the way to every person passing by.

❀

1 July 2006

The air was damp and cold. Aamir stood still, staring at the rows of plants that swayed with the wind. Earlier, when he had arrived, the place bustled with noise and activity; many people had come to pay their respects and offer prayers by folding their hands and bowing before the many plants and trees that were planted to commemorate their loved ones. It grew quieter; almost everyone was leaving on seeing rain-bearing clouds gather in the sky. The sky darkened and flashed with lightning. In another time, in Dhruv's company, he would have enjoyed the sheer excitement and thrill that are a part of rainy nights, but now, he realized he felt numb. It was as if the warmth of life had crept out of his body, leaving him unable to feel. He felt as if he weren't really doing that, being there; as if the whole thing was nothing but a dream or a living nightmare.

Aamir had taken a half-day off at work and driven past the city at noon to get to that place which was located at a hill-top in Lonavla. He'd looked forward to a quiet and solitary night, away from the hustle and bustle of Mumbai. Now, as he stood there, he was filled with overpowering thoughts of doubling back to the city, to Dhruv, to have dinner together. He decided to go with his mind.

'You have to avoid these depressing thoughts. The more attention you give to them, the stronger they grow.' Aamir remembered Anvi's words from one of their conversations.

Anvi. His girlfriend; his everything.

Although he tried to do what Anvi have suggested, his sense of loneliness got the better of him.

Aamir took one last look at the trees, smiled sadly and then went to his car. He fastened his seatbelt and turned the key in the ignition. The next thing he knew, he was driving speedily towards the city. He thought of Dhruv, who was to reach home in a few hours. Aamir wanted to get home before Dhruv. The word *home* always brought a picture of his parents to his mind…his parents who had overburdened him too early in life, with too many responsibilities.

'I think of you all the time, mom and dad. I picture us together every night before I force myself to fall asleep. No matter what I do for Dhruv, I know that it will never be enough. Yet, I am trying. I try to keep him happy and make him a better person like you'd have wanted him to be. But how long could I be a parent to him? How could I be as caring, tender and patient with him, mom, when you listened to him and calmed his temper? How could I ever watch over him with your precision, dad, when he does something good and when he does something wrong? If only you were here with both of us, I wouldn't have to think about any of it. You'd have taken care of both of us. If only I had a chance to learn more from you!'

Aamir felt as if he was moving through life without any reason. The mere sight of families spending time together made him lose his composure. Even after so many years, he couldn't accept the fact that his parents weren't there with them. Every once in a while, he would call for them and wait for them to respond and talk to him. He longed to hear their voices. He craved to see them, to be with them. He felt as if he had been swallowed by nothingness. He prayed incessantly for his parents to come back, in some form. He kept on living with more unanswered questions, unheard prayers and unfulfilled expectations. The time they had spent together had been the happiest in his life.

Aamir reached his apartment in Andheri (East) on time. He got out of the car and glanced up at the balcony to see if Dhruv was back. He unlocked the door to his flat and stepped inside, tossed his things on the bed and made his way to the bathroom to freshen up. Then, lying in bed with the bedside lamp on, he closed his eyes, lost in thought. Twenty minutes later, he reached for his phone and called up Dhruv, who was already late. Dhruv didn't respond.

He prepared some tea for himself and then texted Dhruv because he felt anxious. He didn't receive a reply this time too. It was two hours past the time Dhruv usually returned from work, and he wasn't replying to any of his calls or messages. Without wasting any time, he got into his car, feeling worried, wondering if everything was all right. He called Dhruv's office switchboard while driving, but according to the night shift staff, Dhruv had left the office three hours ago. Breathing heavily, he walked up to Dhruv's friend Raghav's apartment on the third floor in Vile Parle to check if he was there, but nobody seemed to know anything.

As the minutes passed, Aamir felt his heart tremble with horror. He suddenly became conscious of the tingling of his nerves, the sensation of something crawling on his skin, and a chilling of his blood though he was sweating in the humidity. He couldn't begin to comprehend where Dhruv had gone and wondered if he was with Vratika. Aamir tried her number, but that too went unanswered. He was having a difficult time fighting his intuitions as the night grew darker. He stopped and bent over for some time. He grabbed the car keys again and drove to Carter Road, Bandra. He slowed his car to get a clearer view. For the next few hours, he visited all his and Dhruv's friends and acquaintances, but it was all in vain. He was clueless.

After searching for almost three hours, he drove back home, feeling hopeless. He started calling and messaging all his friends to see if anybody had been in touch with Dhruv.

When he got no positive response, he decided to wait for Dhruv to come home.

It was already midnight and Dhruv had not yet come home. Not knowing what else to do, he turned off the lights, shut the door and grabbed his car keys to drive to the police station nearby. He felt like crying; his hands were shaking and he felt extremely unsettled. He reached the car and suddenly saw a man who was walking haphazardly towards him, looking like an idiot; tall, built-up, short hair, hefty arms and a lost look on his face.

It was Dhruv.

Dhruv came closer. He was having trouble walking straight. He'd wanted to keep his mind sharp when he met Aamir, but his head had begun to pound and he'd been sick to his stomach. His vision was blurring. Everybody was staring at him. He belched loudly as he walked up to Aamir, tripped over a piece of junk on the street and blacked out as he fell on Aamir's shoulder.

Aamir held Dhruv's shoulder steadily. He was relieved to see him, but worried and angry too. They slowly walked back to their home.

'Can you walk me to my room?' Dhruv asked in a strange voice.

'Thank you for this, Dhruv. You just did the unexpected. I'd better get back; I've got an early morning tomorrow.' Aamir's tone expressed his disappointment and anger. It wasn't the first time he'd disappointed Aamir this way.

For the first time ever, Dhruv narrowed his eyes at Aamir. 'Don't do this,' he said.

'Do what? Tell you how I feel now? Tell the truth? Why? It won't change anything. You won't change your persistent ability to turn a deaf ear to whatever I say. That's what you always do. You hurt me. Go ahead! It doesn't mean anything to you anyway. Do you even care about anything…anything at all?'

Dhruv was silent.

'I didn't mean it.' Aamir replied, his voice soft. 'I was so worried about you first, and then upset after seeing you in that drunken state that I took it out on you. You were absent all evening and I was extremely anxious.'

'I miss mom and dad. I have almost no memories of them.'

'I know, Dhruv. I too miss them like you do. But they're right here with us and we both should value what we have right now. More than anything, I want you to talk to me about everything in this world.'

Dhruv nodded, again without meeting Aamir's eyes and smiled weakly.

Aamir put his arm around Dhruv's shoulder. Dhruv seemed to accept that, but he knew he had more to say.

'You don't like your job, your boss? Don't go there. Take a break. You don't have to do it necessarily.' Aamir patted Dhruv's shoulder.

'Then I'll be jobless, useless and bored to death, roaming around in a meaningless life,' Dhruv said with clear despair in his voice.

'I would never think that about you.'

'No. You never would. I know that.'

'Then what is it? Why do I get the feeling you're not telling me something?'

'There's nothing to tell.'

'I know there is.' Then, in a tone of sudden understanding, Aamir said at once, 'It's about Vratika, right?'

Knowing he couldn't hide the truth from Aamir anymore, Dhruv replied, 'Yes, it's about her. She fought with me for not turning up at dinner at the decided time as I was totally stuck up in a meeting in office. When I reached a little late and apologized for it, she made a scene in front of everyone in the restaurant. She always fails to understand me, but I just can't think of living without her. She knows this and takes undue advantage. If I feel hurt or disappointed about something and speak to her about it, she always finds it inappropriate, immature or meaningless. She never hears me out. Perhaps that's why she understands nothing about me, despite all these years of togetherness. I feel empty and alone. I don't know where I am going with her. It's like sailing a ship with no directions. I feel ashamed of saying all this.'

The room was silent as they sat alone with their thoughts. Aamir broke the silence, 'It's not only what happens to you that determines your happiness, brother; it also has to do with how you think about what happened to you and how much that matters to you. If you still love her, love her generously, care deeply and always speak kindly without any expectations. Everything will fall into place eventually…if it's meant to be.'

He paused, waiting for Dhruv to say something, but he stayed silent, deep in his thoughts.

'But if you don't feel like being with her for any reason, move on! Let her know, have no concern for tomorrow and never bang on that closed door ever again. It's going to be challenging, but you might sense a new world then. You're happy or unhappy because of what you think, feel and do. The moment passes. We walk on and so does everybody else.'

'I'm sorry. I don't even know what I did and said tonight. But that was very conscientious of you. I am glad to have you as a brother. Thanks for having me back.'

'Just try to do as I say and it will be better soon, I promise.' Aamir smiled for the first time in hours, nodding his head in assurance. 'Have you had dinner yet?'

'No,' Dhruv replied.

'Would you like to have your favourite white sauce pasta right now before we go off to sleep?'

'It sounds delicious; I'd love it.' He grinned. 'Thank you for everything, especially for planning a special dinner tonight, brother. This is the best day we've spent together...talking after a long time,' Dhruv added.

Aamir returned Dhruv's smile. 'Thank you for coming back, Dhruv,' he fought back his tears and whispered to himself.

Minutes ticked by, long minutes. Dhruv rushed towards the restaurant as soon as he got out from office. Vratika wasn't picking up the call now. But he hoped to see her there. He reached the restaurant, usually very crowded owing to its popularity for amazing food and drinks. He had shown up an hour late. He saw Vratika had started drinking without him.

'I'm sorry. I didn't do this intentionally,' he said defensively. 'I just got stuck in an unplanned meeting in office.'

'So you decided to ignore my calls and enjoy my waiting here for you?' Vratika said, clearly disgusted.

'Come on, you can't pin this one on me. I was supposed to reach here in time, sweetheart. I couldn't respond to your calls for a reason.'

'Wait, your supposition has nothing to do with the reality, Mr. Dhruv. Don't give me this crap. Do you get that?'

'You don't understand.'

'That's insane. You've simply kept me waiting here for god knows how long and you're giving me this shit of not understanding you, Dhruv. Screw you,' she said, gripping her glass tight.

'Listen, Vratika. You've to act sensible now if you don't want to worsen it. I've acted sensible when you expected me to. I expect the same from you here. People are looking here. Don't create a scene please.'

Vratika knocked the glass over, pushed the table in anger which caused many heads to turn towards their table. 'Give me one such example, Dhruv. I bet you. Give me one right now.'

The restaurant manager was standing on a side and saw this conversation getting worse.

'I'm sure you don't want to go there.'

'I said, give me one example right now.'

'Alright! Then do me a favour and think about your birthday night, when I caught you getting laid with your ex and still understood it.'

Vratika's face turned red and eyes burnt in anger; she slapped him tight on his face.

The manager had no way to find out what the conversation was about, but gathered that trouble was brewing. He rushed towards them and pushed Dhruv out of the restaurant in disgust and anger. 'Take this shit outside the restaurant and make sure he doesn't stand around. Else call the cops and get him arrested,' he shouted as the bouncers followed his advice.

Dhruv, hesitating, finally turned away from the faces staring at him. It took him no more than a minute to pass that street where he had just been insulted by his girlfriend, who knew well that Dhruv couldn't live without her.

For the entire next week, they didn't talk, before Dhruv apologized to her again for reasons unknown to him and everybody else who knew about that night's incident. He was relieved that Vratika had picked up his 57th call and also agreed to go out with him for a movie by the weekend, as offered by Dhruv in sheer excitement.

In a way, Dhruv stopped living his life his own way and became a puppet who danced to Vratika's tone. He refused to hear his inner voice and was always a giver in this so-called one-sided relationship.

9 July 2006

Aamir arrived at his flat much before his usual time. He made himself a cup of tea and sat in the balcony. He always loved evenings like that. He took his bag and put it in a corner. Feeling a little uncertain, he took a picture out of the bag and held it delicately in his hands. He couldn't help leaning forward and embracing the picture between his arms and chest, as if it were a person. He closed his eyes and whispered to himself, 'You're always going to be missed.'

Aamir's thoughts were interrupted by the squeaking of the door. Dhruv peered into the balcony. 'I saw your car outside. I wanted to make sure that everything was okay.' He said by way of explanation. 'I didn't expect you back so soon; it being the quarter end today.'

When Aamir didn't respond, Dhruv walked in and immediately spotted a picture in Aamir's hand from a distance. 'You okay, brother?' He asked cautiously.

'Yes,' Aamir replied despondently.

'Missing your girl? Why don't you go and meet her then? Something is wrong, isn't it?'

Aamir looked thoughtful for a moment. 'It's quite a distance to travel and I'm tired already. I think I was a little rough on her. I'll sort it out and meet her soon. Don't worry.'

'Are you sure?'

'Yes, as sure as I can be,' Aamir said.

'Aamir, you haven't talked about her much to me. And when I asked about her, you felt a pang of missing her too. I could see that. I'd like to help you with a suggestion: get married to her. What do you say?' He smiled as he said this.

'I understand what you're saying, Dhruv,' he said. 'But I want you to know that it's difficult for us to get married for certain reasons. Plus, I'm not willing to make any false promises that I am not able to fulfil tomorrow.'

'Not a good response. At least not as good as you usually are in convincing me. You can't fake, Aamir,' he said calmly.

'Forget it! We'll discuss it some other day. Right now, there's something much more important and you need to know about it.' Aamir smiled as he leaned over and pulled an envelope out of his bag.

'What's that?'

'Close your eyes,' Aamir said, 'and I'll tell you about it.' Dhruv did as he was asked to and heard the envelope being unwrapped. 'Okay, you can have it in your hands and see it now.'

Dhruv opened his eyes to a railway ticket for two to Kanhal. Aamir's face was buoyant. 'We're going to our hometown Brahmi after reaching Kanhal.'

Dhruv nodded, feeling uninterested, not wanting to say anything.

Aamir smiled broadly as he said, 'It's our parents' anniversary in some days, and I want to celebrate it in Brahmi this time. I think you'll understand. It's been almost twenty years already and both of us do miss them a lot, don't we? Didn't you like the surprise?'

'Yeah, right. There's no denying that, but don't you think it'll bring back so much at once and set the whole memory thing up yet again.'

'Sure, it would. But we're not strangers to Brahmi. Our parents lived there; we had a home and a life. Twenty years is a long time...too long. I don't know if we'll ever do it again after this, but for once, we have to go back and live in Brahmi for our parents, even if it's for a week.'

Dhruv knew how Aamir felt about that place, but then, he also knew how much it disturbed him at times.

'I am being rather silly, am I not?' Aamir asked, trying to smile.

'What do you mean?'

'This whole thing! Sudden plans to travel to Brahmi out of the blue. Got the tickets done already. You must be thinking I've gone crazy.'

'Come on! You know very well I would not think like that. Though I don't know how *I* feel, I can see how *you* feel about it and that makes it worth a shot,' Dhruv said.

Aamir was really happy to get such a supportive and mature response from his little brother. He was sure that everything would turn out fine. Both of them had always been too busy to ever go there, but somewhere he knew, they were actually running away from their past. They never felt ready to bring back the memories of those days. But now, Aamir wanted to face it. He wanted to absorb all that he once had abandoned.

'Would you mind telling me something about Brahmi - our life, our home there?' Dhruv asked Aamir.

'Listen, I have spent a lot of time travelling today anyway. Just the thought of talking about Brahmi delights me. But are you sure you're not going out with Vratika tonight?' Aamir teased.

'No, she's busy and I am all ears.'

Aamir was quiet for a moment as he picked up his cup of tea, aware of the stillness in the moment. 'I hope I can describe what Brahmi was like at that time. You haven't spent a lot of time there. It is a beautiful place, with the mists rising and blue skies and cool breezes and birds chirping on trees with shimmering leaves. When we go there, you will remember the past, our family…you will see the real Brahmi then.'

He sighed, closed his eyes for a moment, feeling more alive than he had felt in a long time and continued, 'Ah, Brahmi! I wonder if I can truly ever leave it behind me. I bet you don't have a view like that anywhere else in the world. Most of the people there were farmers; it's located in the hills, fifteen kilometres away from Kanhal. It's too far in the interior to catch the attention of those who are unaware of its existence. I don't think I would find it changed. A big empty sky, broken sunlight that passes through the leaves of water oaks and giant trees, some hundred feet high, illuminating the colours of autumn, and a beautiful lake with hundreds of swans, just a kilometre ahead on the main road. Then you will see a majestic oak tree on the banks of the river. When you sit there, you'll see many birds chirping and flying around, as if they have no intention to settle down. You feel revitalized by the fresh and cool air of Brahmi as it touches you gently, occasionally bringing water droplets…I cannot express it in words. You can actually feel yourself flying in the air forever. You can listen to the music of the river flowing nearby and sing along. It's heavenly.'

Seeing Dhruv's face relax as he spoke, Aamir simply carried on. 'You move ahead on the main road and see a green, dense forest, stretched far on either side of the road. It's an exotic world filled with purple flowers, unusual scents and unique plants. It's a peaceful world, probably the only place without anger, violence and any expectations. A few families lived in Brahmi, including ours. Our home, built of wood, was surrounded by big trees. It was a bungalow-style home, untouched by the outside world, as if hiding itself to avoid impurity. It's still unchanged. You can't afford to miss the beauty of a sunrise or a full moon day from the temple and that huge tree located so close to it. They say it makes your life worthwhile when you see natural gold water the first thing in the morning. You can make a wish and watch it come true. That moment surely works its magic. It's as if you're standing at god's side, alongside your soul, guiding yourself towards a beautiful future.

'Brahmi gives you memories worth cherishing forever. It makes you believe that there will come a time when you'll eventually be an integral part of it. There's something which makes you want to spend time there. Once you have lived in Brahmi, it will live on in your memories for ages to come.'

He stayed silent for long time, as if trying hard to bring himself back to the present. He took a deep breath and held it for a moment, hoping he could return to the past and go back twenty years, longing for that incident to have never happened, wishing for one more chance. He smiled at Dhruv and said, 'It is heaven. It is home. And, it is different.'

1986

It was a month after their parents' death, but it seemed to go by slowly. Aamir didn't know what to say to Dhruv, since he felt Dhruv was too young to handle it or really understand. For Aamir, their parents' death in the forest was unexpected; he had nothing to look back to in the past. He had no visions of the future; he did not know where they were going, nor did he know how they were to get there. All he knew was that he had to get work and a place to stay in, so that he could care for his little brother.

A couple of humble people showed their support in helping the kids and they got a place to live in. His father's friend, Mr. Das helped them get settled after the catastrophe. After they grew up, Aamir's only purpose was to get enough money to afford food and basic education for both of them on his own. But getting work didn't take away the pain of losing their parents at such an early age. He was aware that he lacked a mother's care and a father's guidance in his life. But he could still smile, take Dhruv sightseeing in Mumbai and instil in Dhruv a belief for a wonderful future ahead.

When Dhruv asked about their parents, Aamir would nod and tell him that they were on a long journey to a different world and they were always there to help them as they have helped earlier in getting them a place to live in and work to earn their living. He kept telling his little brother that their parents wanted both of them to be happy, and that the happier their lives were, the sooner they will come to meet them.

Things still hadn't been sorted out, but with Dhruv growing up, it became easier for Aamir to focus on more things, get a better job and a more suitable place for them to stay. He thought things were getting better as both of them began their studies again. Moreover, they had grown used to living without their parents. Even though people around him said that they seemed to be doing better, Aamir often sat alone, thinking about the truth. To him, nothing would ever be the same again. He thought it was really impossible for him to find someone else who could take his parents' place. He decided to never get married and made Dhruv's happiness the only purpose of his life.

In his dreams, he often saw himself on the lakeside with his parents and Dhruv. It was a bright day, the sunlight reflecting off the water. As he walked along the banks of the lake with his parents, he listened intently as they told him about his life, Dhruv's life and a beautiful life lying ahead. They told him that he needed to take care of all of it. Finally, after some hesitation, he agreed to everything they said. He didn't want them to leave, but he watched as they slowly faded away. He found himself straining to remember everything about that moment. They turned and said, 'Goodbye, take care, and we love you both.'

He had lost count of the number of times he had seen this dream.

March, 2005

They watched the sun go down, bleeding red on the high skyscrapers of Mumbai. They waited till the stars started coming out one by one and had dinner under the night sky. It was getting late, but it didn't really bother Anvi. All she did was to bask in the glory of a beautifully spent day. She suggested walking along the nearby beach. 'It's really beautiful at night,' he said. She agreed. The night was mild. As they walked over the beach, she felt the sea breeze in her face and smiled back. They walked for a while, barefoot, hands entwined, as they stared across the moonlit waves dancing and crashing against the sand on the shore.

'I haven't had this perfect a night ever. I wish it to last forever.' Aamir embraced Anvi.

She replied softly, 'So do I.'

She leaned towards him as she realized that she hadn't said much since they'd started their day. 'Tell me, Aamir, what do you remember most from the time we've spent together?'

'Everything.'

'Anything in particular?'

'No,' he said.

'You don't remember?'

He answered after a quiet moment, very seriously. 'I do remember, and I meant it when I said 'everything'. I can't really pick any one time that meant more than any other, and in all the time that we've spent together, there has always been something wonderful; worth cherishing for the rest of my life. Our relationship is probably as pure as it's ever been. Before you came into my life, I was tired of always being alone.'

'You mean to say I was in the right place at the right time?'

He shook his head. 'I didn't mean it to sound like that. I don't think I would've had such a lovely time with anybody else in this world. Besides, being with you has made me a better person, a better lover. The days spent with you have been the best days of my life.'

Anvi stood still, looking intently into his eyes. He returned her gaze lovingly, which seemed to pierce Anvi's heart. No one had ever said such beautiful things to her before. She knew why she was so much in love with Aamir. She didn't know what to say and stayed silent. The sand was cool beneath her feet.

They walked together quietly some more before they decided to sit. There were a few others on the beach by now, though they were far away and Anvi couldn't see anything but shadows.

Aamir had got wooden logs and started the fire, and it changed the moment to purely romantic. Winds were blowing faster and his face was glowing in the burning flames. Neither of them needed words for what they were feeling. They had come much farther than this. As they were re-arranging logs, Anvi gave him a shy smile and they continued to look at each other for a while before they spotted a couple standing nearby, observing how beautifully they were doing all this.

'Aamir, remember when you first proposed to me and disclosed your feelings?' Anvi smiled and asked.

'Yes.'

'Why did you hesitate?'

He looked at her curiously. 'What do you mean?'

'Don't get me wrong, Aamir. I respect you for what you are, always had, and always would. But, I mean, you looked almost like you regretted it the moment you said it.'

He shrugged. 'I'm not sure that regret is the word I'd like to use. I think I was more worried about your career as crime reporter along with my other responsibilities. Dhruv. But I didn't regret it.'

'Are you sure?'

'Yes, I'm very certain. You have to remember that Dhruv was studying at that time; he was yet to start working, so my mind drifted and I started thinking about his life. I've watched him crying alone, and without a word. It's difficult to be with him. He has never experienced our parents' love. He has seen such sights as a child! I keep worrying – what if he no longer thinks positively of our relationship after knowing of your crime reporting career, along with the life risk involved in it, and he assumes that it wouldn't be too favourable a thing for our family if I marry you. That's why I often avoid talking to him about you.'

'I know you both care so much about each other. You are the only thing he has left as a family, and it is the same for you. He's quite justified in not being able to accept his fate. I won't ever expect him to understand the loss of his parents at such an early age! I understand your part here too. Trust me on this. But...do you think you'll ever be able to marry me?

'I don't know. Why?'

'Because, I was hoping you would.'

In the distance, he could see the lights and she felt his hand moving against hers.

'Would you make dinner for me if we get married?' He smiled to lighten the moment and there was so much he wanted to say to her, but he knew from everything wonderful they discussed that evening that it wasn't the right time to discuss it.

'I'd cook anything that you want in the world.' She laughed.

'Then I'll consider it, I promise.'

'Then, you should bring Dhruv along sometime. Let us get to know each other.'

'I know. I will, soon, and I bet you'd like him.'

'Undoubtedly.'

They walked the full length of the beach, exchanging stories from work. He stood close to her, their shoulders barely touching.

'What are you thinking?' she asked.

'Just that I didn't think it was possible to love someone as much as I love you,' he whispered, running his finger down her cheek.

'I didn't think it was possible for me either. You know, love being overrated and all,' she answered with a little laugh.

'Will you make me a promise?' she asked seriously.

'Anything you want,' he said earnestly.

'You'll try your best, make an effort to explain things to Dhruv and marry me. I am sure he'll understand everything and would like to see his brother happy, just as you wish the same for him.'

Aamir took a moment to answer. 'I do promise you, Anvi. That's the least I can do for our happiness.' As he said this, he took her hand in his. She had long, slender fingers, and beautiful, graceful hands.

She smiled tenderly and Aamir lifted her hands as he kissed her softly on the lips; he leaned in slowly and kissed her again and she kissed back, feeling delighted at the wonderful time they had spent together.

'I love you, Anvi. More than you can ever imagine. I always have and I always will. You're dearest to me. I am glad that we spent such a beautiful evening after a long time,' he said. He was obviously taken away in love with her, and it pleased her no end.

'Oh, Aamir,' she said. She wanted him, needed him more than ever now. The world seemed dreamlike to both of them that night. There was such a gentleness and softness to her that he always wanted to see in her girl. He hugged her with all his love and a regret that he hadn't found her years before.

July 2005

He'd seen her on television a few minutes earlier. It'd been a long time since they last met, partly because of Anvi's career as a crime reporter. They had been longing to meet that day. It was Sunday, four days after the encounter with a gang of criminals who the police had finally shot down. He still looked utterly worn out but was grateful that he was going to meet Anvi. Aamir had a hard time when Anvi couldn't pick up his call. He could not sleep for the fear that she had been hurt in those criminal attacks. Whether or not they would ever walk together again remained a question in his mind. It was a subject that Aamir and Anvi had avoided so far.

He was sitting in the balcony and smiled when he saw her walk into his building.

'Do you feel all right?' Anvi enquired as she entered Aamir's flat and noticed that he looked more frail and pale.

'I was worried for you, but I am good now, and was just about to open a bottle of wine. Would you like a glass?' He asked, sounding depressed. He did not seem to be in a rush to discuss anything at the moment. He had rarely touched her, kissed her or hugged her in the last few days. The last time he was affectionate with her was some months back at the beachside.

'Please,' she said and looked absolutely exhausted. She glanced around for food and saw some fruits lying there.

He reached for the bottle and the corkscrew as she sat down.

For the past four days, he had wondered what it would be like to get married to her. He knew that the attacks could have been far worse for her. His life would have been paralyzed.

'How is Dhruv?' She asked as Aamir gave her a glass of wine. She could see that he was anxious and tense.

'He's fine. He's gone on a road trip with his friends to Goa,' he said, sounding worried.

'Don't worry; he's a grown-up now. He can take care of himself,' she said firmly and cheerfully.

'Yes, I know. Anyway, things must have changed a lot for you in the past week. You never really stopped working. I was going crazy sitting here, watching television, knowing about the terrorist attacks and your being out there.' He was unusually serious as he said those words.

'I understand your concern, Aamir. But this is something that none of us can do anything about. It's my job. Yes, at first I was scared, contemplating whether I could even make it home alive, but now I am past that. I've got to do what I am supposed to do. I really need you to be on board with this, all right?'

'But you can't do this all your life. Your taking such risks terrifies me, Anvi.'

'I've got nothing better to do and I've toiled so hard to do the work that I am doing now. I am serving a greater cause, much bigger than our individual lives. And there are no free lunches, you know that.'

'To be honest, I think you don't understand my point. Are you sure of our relationship and marriage? Where exactly do I come into your greater bigger picture?'

'How can you say that? If this is the level of understanding you have of me, about us, then I think we should be grateful that we aren't married yet,' she spoke indignantly and shot him an accusing look. She was totally flabbergasted to hear what he had just said.

Aamir shook his head and clenched his fists. His expressions reflected his fear and concern. He had wanted to talk to Anvi about this for quite some time but always postponed the conversation, looking for a better moment. This was not the message he had hoped to convey to her. 'I am sorry, baby. It wasn't meant to go like this. It is my fear speaking. I can't afford to lose you, even if it is for some great cause. Yes, I am being selfish, but I deserve some happiness. You are my happiness. I can't spend my life wondering every day whether you'll make it back home.'

'This is no time to hide behind words, Aamir.'

'This isn't about hiding behind words, Anvi. I care for you, and I see nothing wrong if I get worried about the profession that you've chosen to pursue. These attacks and crimes in our country have now got me worried. I don't want you to leave your profession or anything like that; you have your own life and I have mine. I am nobody to comment upon it. But I would ask you to try and shift into news anchoring, if that interests you. I've lost enough people in my life. I don't want to lose somebody whom I love the most now. I won't be able to handle it. Do you understand me now?' he said, sipping his drink.

'I have things to do, Aamir. Even if I understand your logic here, there's nothing that I can do about it. I so want to settle down myself. And let's consider I give up on what I am doing. Isn't that another way to support the very heinous activities against which I stand today? You have got every right to be worried about me, to counter my view...and you're not entirely wrong either. But running away from responsibility or handing it over to somebody else isn't really what I would wish to do. Isn't that the very thing that makes you love me the most? Remember, you said it yourself?'

Aamir couldn't disagree. He already knew he couldn't make Anvi give up her job. Part of him was already feeling guilty for trying to turn her mind against the very thing he loved about her.

He knew they lived in a country where armchair critics on social media sites blamed the government of the day for everything that went wrong. Everyone talked of rights, but no one spoke of responsibilities and duties. 'It is not the criminals or gangsters or terrorists that are the threat to our nation. The real threat is the attitude of the people. I want to make a difference, even if it is the tiniest thing ever done. I'd rather die like a dog on the street, but not of a heart attack, watching TV at home.'

Painful silence followed for some time before he spoke, 'I am sorry for putting you in this situation. I am there for you, Anvi, in all your decisions.' Aamir sounded apologetic, yet concerned.

'Aamir, stop getting so worried. I don't have any future plans to get myself killed, okay? Now take that expression off your face. It is killing me. We'll work everything out very soon.'

'I know we will.' Aamir took her in his arms and held her tight. 'I am never going to let you go. You are mine.'

'Yes, I am,' she said with tears filling her eyes.

It wasn't easy for either of them, but they had gotten used to the life they were living. It hurt him thinking about her being so far away from him when he wanted her to be safe and protected. He hated being so far away, not being able to watch her, take care of her, talk to her. But the time that they had spent together was the happiest of their lives. He had countless wishes of the life they could have together, yet he could not stop worrying.

'I'll call you at every chance I get, Aamir. That's a promise,' she said, ruffling his hair.

'Do you swear you'll call me?' he asked.

'I told you, it's a promise.' She threw her arms around his neck and attempted to strangle him again as he laughed at her. 'I promise, Aamir. I promise, I'll be a good girl and give you no reason to get worried and I'll try and shift into news anchoring after I serve my purpose well here.'

'We'll see that. But listen, do not mess with anybody and don't invite trouble. It is not your business to put your cute little nose in everyone else's business. You got that?'

'Aye, aye, captain,' she said with a crooked grin, with one hand around his neck and one hand saluting.

'It's so good to see you smiling,' he said, putting his arm around her waist and kissing her passionately. He was tempted to ask if she could stay for the night.

'Yes, and this is good too. Now you stop your hunger strike as I can't see you on this pitifully small appetite. Eat lots and make more love with me,' she said in a muffled voice, winked and kissed him back with more passion.

Now that she was home safely, he was going to put all his efforts into getting all those beautiful moments back where they'd been till some months back. They lay next to each other in silence for an hour. Being with each other was all that mattered to them. Anvi then spoke again, 'How is Dhruv doing?'

'He isn't doing well. He caught Vratika with her ex some days ago. She was insisting that she'd never met this person in the past few years before Dhruv forced her to confess.'

'Is he still talking to her?'

'I guess, yes. After she swore many times that she won't be meeting her ex ever again.'

'Dhruv is either too crazy or just too blind to see through that girl's behaviour now. Remember, the last time I told you about that girl sitting so cosily with some other guy? You simply disconnected there.'

'Anvi, I was certain you were telling it as you saw it, but there's nothing in the world that would make Dhruv see it. He's in love with her. He's obviously far too stubborn to understand that.'

Aamir and Anvi both knew that Vratika was not in love with Dhruv. She didn't even care to respect his feelings. She was simply toying with him. She was responsible for Dhruv's bad mood swings and terrible habits.

'You must speak to him.'

'He'll be here in a couple of days. I'll see how he feels and then speak. But then, I can't really promise anything. Vratika has become a habit for him and that would be hard to break.'

'I understand. Don't overstress yourself. You've done a wonderful job with Dhruv. I hope he understands; I'd like that to happen very much indeed,' she said.

Aamir nodded. And they walked to the balcony at the back, which had a beautiful view of tall trees and an open skyline. The wind was gently brushing the loosened strands of her hair. They stood beneath the stars. It was a perfect moment for them. As they put on some beautiful music, their bodies felt like one. They slowly moved their feet to the music and the songs were magical enough to make the moment all the more special. Neither of them spoke for a long time; they just held each other close and danced. It was a beautiful and warm night and they were smiling while enjoying the moment. Anvi wasn't sure what had made her agree to Aamir's proposal that day, but that surely made her life worth living.

'Aamir, I do dream of getting married to you someday. I don't know what tomorrow might bring, but I'll love you the same for the rest of my life and even after that.'

It was something that he was absolutely certain about. 'I love you, Anvi.' He whispered as he held her close to him. 'So very much.' And as he said the words, he kissed her and put his arms around her; time just seemed to melt. All he knew was he had never been as happy as that night in his life and he never wanted this moment to end. They were kissing each other and making love like never before. They both longed for the warmth and closeness they had shared.

The night ended quietly, with the two of them asleep in each other's arms.

11 July 2006

'Are you all right brother?' Dhruv woke up as he heard a scream.

'Y...yes. I just had a bad dream . I'll be okay. It's fine,' Aamir explained.

Dhruv moved towards him and asked with eyes half-open, 'You saw the same dream again?'

'No, this was different. I told you I'll be fine; don't worry.'

Though Aamir told Dhruv not to worry, he had the feeling that something wasn't right. He was scared for some reason and it upset him more as he thought about it. Furious, he made a cup of tea for himself and stepped onto the balcony. He checked the time. It was five in the morning. He always rose at the crack of dawn, but it was too early that day. He stared at the sky in wonder, amazed that the darkness hid so much which the sunrise would reveal in an hour.

Aamir could feel something twisting and tightening in his chest. He wanted to talk about something, he did not know why. He was afraid, although he tried to pooh-pooh it away. As he finished his tea, he picked up his personal diary and began writing in it, with an uneasy expression on his face, as if he was hit by a reality that he had avoided for years.

At around 9.00 a.m., as Dhruv stepped onto the balcony after he got ready for office, he saw Aamir still writing in his diary. He sat in the balcony with Aamir.

'Dhruv, how's everything with Vratika now?' Aamir asked.

'It's ok. why? What happened?' he replied.

'Because I sort of figured out it isn't when you were trying to convince her for something last night and she disconnected your call abruptly. It isn't even ten days to that night and it's happening again,' he said.

'We've got plenty of discussions happening these days. I am sure we'll sort it out soon.'

'She's ruling you. I hope you know that, Dhruv. You should really be smart in dealing with that girl.'

'I didn't ask your opinion on this, Aamir. So please don't start preaching. How would you feel if I do the same introspection for you and Anvi?' he said in anger.

'Just forget it, okay? Because you're in no mood to understand my concern here,' Aamir said to Dhruv, sensing his anger.

'It's none of your business, brother. I tell you what - you figure out what problems you have with me and Vratika and let me know what they are someday. Your advices are too much to handle sometimes. Please stop interfering so much,' Dhruv said agitatedly.

'I am not interfering here. I just want to see you happy. Am I expecting too much? I am not asking you to leave her or anything. Just asking you to be more practical and open in your relationship.'

'I don't know what to do about what you want. But this is really pissing me off.' He choked off his words and ran to the living area to find Aamir's car keys.

'Stop!' Aamir called out, trying to keep Dhruv calm.

Aamir shouted, stunned by Dhruv's temperament, breathing heavily. He saw Dhruv pick up his car to drive to office instead of taking his usual bus, as he had been delayed during this discussion.

'*Don't worry! I might be totally wrong in what I said. Drive safe and reach office safely. You forgot to take the car documents; they were lying in my bag.*' Aamir sent a message to Dhruv after he had left.

As soon as Dhruv reached his office, he got a call from Vratika. 'Hey Dhruv, can you come down to Dadar and give me twenty-five thousand in cash this evening?' Vratika asked.

Dhruv was startled by Vratika's sudden demand. He breathed deeply and said, 'Of course, I can give it to you, but it won't be possible for me to come today.'

'Why can't you come?'

'I am meeting someone senior at work today. I might get late and I don't want to keep you waiting like last time. If you want, you can come here and pick it up. But what's the urgency?'

'I can't come. I have my classes and I have to fill up forms for my semester here. That's the urgency.'

'But you asked your parents to send you the fee, right?'

'Yes, but I just finished it all in my shopping and I just realized that. I am just asking you to lend me some money. That's it. I'll return it to you as soon as I make my arrangements.'

'But I can't really come out of office today. It's almost impossible for me.'

'What do you mean? I can't risk my semester here. I don't know anything. You manage it somehow and reach here at the earliest.'

'I don't know what to say to make you understand, darling.'

'There's nothing you can say; that's the only thing I am asking you for because it's urgent. Why don't you understand?'

'Okay! I'll manage and get it, somehow. See you. Bye. Love you.'

Dhruv described the entire situation to Aamir in sheer exasperation over call and also apologized for behaving so badly with him in the morning and taking his car without even asking him.

Aamir could sense there had been an argument.

'You don't need to say sorry. I do understand. And yes, I think I can manage it this evening. My boss is out and I can leave work early,' Aamir offered his help.

He would not hear of Dhruv putting his meeting with the senior person in his company at risk to sort out Vratika's finances. Dhruv wanted to change his department at work and had been waiting to meet the senior man for a very long time.

Aamir said with a smile, 'Cheer up! Soon we're going to have a great vacation in Brahmi. Everything's going to be wonderful.'

Dhruv smiled after what seemed like a long time. 'Yeah, we sure will have a great time.'

'If you need anything else, just call me up. I am about to leave for office.'

Dhruv remained silent. He could not help thinking about how Aamir always made it so easy for him. He seemed to know exactly what to say and do to make him feel better.

'Now don't make faces in your office; give me a hug when we meet. Your brother isn't too difficult to be convinced. We'll dine at your favourite place in Bandra tonight.'

Dhruv wanted to hug Aamir just then. But he vowed to do that when they met for dinner. 'Let me know when you're done with meeting Vratika. I'll reach Bandra directly and after dinner, we can probably go for a walk on Carter Road,' Dhruv said, now pretty relaxed.

Aamir smiled and went to the kitchen, saying, 'I was hoping you would say that. I'll call in the evening.'

As Aamir took a return local to Bandra, he reached the first class compartment and called Dhruv, twice, but in vain. He decided to send him a message.

'Brother, I reached Dadar station on time and called Vratika to collect the money. When she didn't respond to my calls and messages, I decided to visit her flat. She wasn't available there either. I waited for half an hour. I am going to Bandra now. Co-ordinate with her and let me know if I need to visit her again. Stay calm when you speak to her. I am going to buy a jacket for you when I reach Bandra. Waiting for you.'

Dhruv had been in a meeting, unable to take calls. But he managed to read Aamir's sms.

'Aamir visited your flat to give you the money after leaving work early, coz I was busy in office. Where have you been? Why weren't you replying to his messages or calls? Dhruv messaged Vratika frantically.

'Now you know what it feels like to keep others waiting. I so wished it was you. Nonetheless, it was your brother who witnessed it. I never needed any money. You shouldn't have expected me to respond after keeping me waiting that day,' Vratika replied to his text.

Dhruv was enraged. He had been living with her behaviour towards him owing to his love for her. But Aamir having to bear the brunt of it was unacceptable. This had to end.

'*After your behaviour of the past few days, I don't think it's going to work out between us and I owe no explanation for this now. Fuck off,*' Dhruv replied to Vratika angrily.

He simultaneously also wrote an sms to Aamir. '*Sorry brother, it was her plan to get back at me for not meeting her last week and keeping her waiting. Unfortunately, you became her victim. I'll be free soon, reach Carter Road and discuss the rest.*'

His mobile beeped again after a minute. He thought it'd be either Aamir or Vratika. But it was a colleague from office who had left early that day.

'*Mumbai struck by serial blasts. This time they've targeted local trains. Ask your near and dear ones to return home safely and not travel via public transport. Please share this message with everybody you know.*'

It took a moment for him to understand what he had just read. Dhruv was taken aback. He shook his head and came out of the conference room, rushing to the television. The serial blasts were being flashed on all major news channels. His hands started shaking, and body started trembling out of fear.

He remembered that Aamir was travelling to Bandra; he must have taken the local. He called up Aamir, almost panicking. Aamir's phone wasn't reachable. He called up again and messaged too, without receiving a reply.

It was then that his breathing suddenly became difficult. His hands and his body began to shake as he recalled what he had seen of the bomb blast sites on television.

The blast victims were being sent to Hinduja and J.J. Hospital. The hospitals were overflowing. As Dhruv reached Hinduja Hospital after an hour-long traffic jam, he saw the injured brought in for treatment, all of them in a terrible condition. There were thousands of people crying on the roads, in the hospital; the relatives and friends of the deceased were shock-stricken and silent. Distraught family members waited for news of those who were in a serious condition. He heard somebody saying, 'People were jumping out of running trains. When I got off, I saw dead bodies on the tracks and found ten bodies lying in an isolated area. These aren't even in a condition to be identified.'

Pure terror.

Dhruv took a deep breath and told himself that Aamir was all right and nothing had happened to him as he kept searching for him.

But he was scared too, more than he had ever been, because he was sure he would never forgive himself if anything happened to Aamir. There were unsaid words and heavy tears in his eyes. He remembered the conversation with his brother that morning. He knew he was foolish to send his brother to Dadar today. He closed his eyes and wished for the worst nightmare of his life to end. His words came out slurred as he asked people about dead bodies and the mortuary. His eyes were red with unshed tears, his movements unsteady. He took a step ahead, almost losing his balance.

He started checking the bodies and prayed to not find his brother there after that senseless act of violence. He checked three bodies, two of which were difficult to identify as they were burnt badly. He was more worried now. He looked up and saw the doctors giving apologetic replies to family members of many victims. He had never seen anything so terrible before.

He was afraid to see any more bodies; he almost lost his mind as he stared at a brutally attacked, half-burnt body. Tears started rolling down his cheeks. He begged, pleaded and cried beyond limits even at the thought of Aamir being one of those bodies.

In the blink of an eye, his world came crashing down in millions of pieces.

'Aamir!' He screamed it as loud as he could. He was lost. He felt his soul was ripped out of his body. He sat next to hospital's gate and stared at dead bodies with expressions of shock and terror. He felt he had died too after not finding his brother anywhere. He loved his brother deeply, incredibly; so much that he would do anything in the world to get him back. It was his fault. Had he not fought with Aamir that day and not taken his car to office in anger, Aamir wouldn't have travelled by train and faced all this. And if had he not fought with Vratika that day, she wouldn't have tried taking revenge. It could have easily been avoided. His brother would still be alive with him, sitting at Bandra.

He was crying and out of control. This horrific event had turned his life upside down. Little did he know that this glorious day would become the worst nightmare that would profoundly alter his life and devastate his soul.

The police reported that the blasts were caused by bombs, which ripped through passenger compartments in choreographed terrorist attacks on several trains at separate sites.

One piece of footage showed dazed survivors with wounded heads, hands and legs. Another piece of footage claimed it to be the biggest ever attack in Mumbai, where a media channel claimed that they were the first ones to cover the serial blasts news. It also showed the dead bodies of men and women, who were returning home, hoping to spend time with their families. The 11 July attacks would be yet another terrorist incident covered extensively by the media, with few, if any, questions raised by the opposition in the legislature. People would speak of courageous Mumbaikars and the spirit of the city that never sleeps; few would think of the lives of those killed that day, or of the families who had lost a dear one to the blasts. They would light a candle on that day every year, to commemorate a life lost. Politicians the world over would condemn the attacks. And it would be another game played in the parliament.

He wanted to scream, for he had no words to express his sorrow. He lay near the hospital gate after searching for Aamir everywhere possible in Mumbai and calling each of Aamir's friends he knew. He would never forget the terrified expression in a victim's eyes lying beside him, whose body was embedded with shards of iron. He stared at him silently and felt his chest constrict as if he was suffocating.

Dhruv opened his bag and took Aamir's picture out; it was a picture of him and Aamir. As he saw that picture, he wept for his brother, not ready to accept that Aamir was never coming back again. He had lost him, this time forever. There was a fear that grew inside him and almost overpowered him. He was hurt and exhausted – mentally, physically and emotionally.

12 July 2006

It was hard to believe what had happened the past day. The date 11/07 would be etched as a sombre anniversary for the city. But for many, it was something much more personal, and far worse. Newspapers were full of horrifying pictures and showed blood everywhere. People were crying along with their entire families who had lost somebody very close to them. But they say – Mumbai continues to throb.

Dhruv was sleeping beside the hospital's main gate until somebody knocked into him and asked him to wake up and go home. As he woke up, it took him some seconds to realize why he was here and how he had passed out after a stressful night. By the time he got back into the hospital again, he hoped he would get some information about Aamir. He showed the picture to nurses available there. After checking last night records, they coldly rejected. When he persisted and asked some more, the nurses left him alone. He had no idea if he'd ever be able to see him, but he was also a bit relieved in a way that he didn't find Aamir in any of those mortuaries in all the different hospitals where those injured had been sent.

He regained some more strength and called on every number possible which was being displayed on news channels for help. With every call he made to various camps to get some information, he reminded himself to stay positive. He had been battling with his thoughts since last evening and that had been torturous for him. He hadn't, fortunately, got any information about his death from various helpline numbers and they were unsure of the injured ones till then.

'We know this is hard, but we have to ask you a few questions to understand how your brother looks.'

'Will you be able to find him then?'

'We'll try our best,' the gentleman on the other side of the line said and asked a few more questions about his last communication with Aamir. Dhruv answered very patiently.

'What's his age?'

'He just turned 31 in May.'

'Could you give me some general and distinguishing features of him...something which will help us in identifying him?'

It took a few seconds for him to speak. 'He's fair and 5 feet 9 inches tall, 70 kilos or so. Brown hair, brown eyes. He wears specs mostly. He has a mole just above his lips and a birthmark on the forehead.'

'Do you remember what he was wearing?'

He closed his eyes, thinking. But he didn't remember anything.

'No.'

After some minutes of pause, trying not to sound too disappointing, the person at the other end said, 'Sorry. But we've got no information of any such person till now.'

'Maybe you should take a look around once more. I'm very worried as I've got no information about him from anywhere and he was definitely travelling in that train. You've got to help me find by brother,' Dhruv said, worried and panicking.

The man said patiently, 'We understand your situation sir, and have requested more help. We're still gathering more information and some families have been reported missing too. Keep calling every six hours and we'll update you.'

It was obvious to him that this search was going to take a long time and it wasn't going to get any easier. But this whole thing made no sense to him. Whether or not he'd ever be able to see Aamir again still remained a question.

He had two options with him: he could act totally paralyzed and cry over accepting the worst possibility of Aamir being dead; or act as a strong person and do everything to get his brother back if he's alive somewhere. He'd never agree to the first one, so he decided to keep his search on.

For the next week, he kept his search on rigorously and visited all hospitals in Mumbai, gave his picture in newspapers, called the helpline numbers more than a hundred times and visited every government official to seek any kind of help that he oculd get. But, unfortunately, he couldn't get any hint about Aamir or his whereabouts. He had thought again and again about what it would be like to have his brother back in his life.

His heart sank when a policemen informed him that they hadn't been able to find his brother in all those days. He also told Dhruv that he might be dead and must not have been identified by anybody. A few bodies were badly burnt; after receiving no claim to the charred bodies, the government officials had performed the final rituals of all of the bodies collectively. He couldn't believe that his brother had been snatched away from him in those brutal attacks. He lost everything with him. He truly believed he would live through it; he also believed that he'd find him somewhere and he would survive too. He was like a dead man living and ceased to feel anything then. He was traumatized by the information that he got and wasn't willing to believe any of it. But he was standing hopeless, nothingness swooshing over him.

He had lost his brother in a nameless, senseless and mindless killing. It was then that he whispered the most heart-wrecking words of all. 'I am responsible for everything. Had it not been for my ego, my fight with Aamir that day, things would've been different.'

26 July 2006

A lot had changed for him in the last month, but yet, nothing much had changed for the people around him. They still occasionally called him to offer sympathy.

Dhruv was still awake because sleep was an impossibility for him now. Dhruv's innards churned with helplessness and hopelessness. He couldn't remember the last time he had eaten a proper meal or shaved his numb face. In the past week, he had started smoking again and turned to alcohol on the nights when the pain was too unbearable for him to face. His grey hairline showed signs of premature aging and his reddening eyes showed the symptoms of lack of sleep. He couldn't understand his emotions, which changed with each passing moment. He was filled with anger one moment, which quickly transformed into guilt, then gloom, followed by his numerous insecurities and fears of being misunderstood and misjudged for the rest of his life. He felt trapped within the vicious cycle of his own thoughts and was consumed by a hurtful self-questioning that refused to abandon his conscience.

It was now the end of July and Dhruv had just finished explaining Aamir's incident to Mithun. His throat was dry. Mithun was sitting with his head bowed. Dhruv watched him, knowing the suggestions that would come. He needed time to relax and rest. He had been unable to sleep for the past few weeks. He was glad and surprised that Mithun had visited his home to understand why he had absented himself from work. Mithun stood up and pushed the hanging wind chime. When they had met at their workplace, he hadn't spoken much to Dhruv, because he considered him an egoistic person with a bad attitude. Dhruv had never guessed the reason why they never spoke at work; he assumed it was because they were busy with their jobs and had little chance to know each other. Perhaps it was the other night after work, when he saw Dhruv crying like a baby in the men's toilet and trying to hide from the world that broke the wall. He was unable to visit Dhruv's home for many days to offer consolation, because his younger brother was receiving dialysis treatment for his damaged kidneys.

'Are you alright?' Mithun asked.

'You shouldn't be here,' Dhruv said. 'You shouldn't have come. I am just not talking to anybody. You have no idea what I've been through.'

'It's a little late to think about it now,' Mithun said.

'You have to go.'

'Just like that? Remember, you need somebody to talk to, it's good to accept help from people sometimes, even from strangers, if you consider me one,' Mithun said.

'What are you doing here, Mithun? I am the culprit here. You shouldn't be talking to me.' Dhruv drank the last of his wine and pushed the glass aside.

'I've been around enough to know that you can't do this intentionally. It was just an accident,' Mithun said. 'But as a friend, I've never been one to impose. I believe you need some time alone.' Mithun said, as he reached the front door.

'How did you know I was here? I don't really know what you're trying to tell me.'

'Well, since my own life is in the dumps, I could understand what one goes through when life plays it rough. I just asked for your address from our HR department and thought of walking in. When I arrived here, the house was dark but the door wasn't locked. So, I took a chance.'

Dhruv took a deep breath, trying to make sense of Mithun's rambling. 'Is that really what you wanted to talk about, Mithun?'

'Yes, I saw you crying a few times in the past week. I was there, in the washroom. It's so unlike you. And after that you stopped coming to work. I was worried. I have been observing you, and it is no exaggeration to say that you seem more than upset. You are like my younger brother. He's a lot like you, in fact, and I've seen my younger brother facing a lot of pain. He's dying every day. He's on a support system and getting dialysis thrice a week. I know how it feels to see somebody close dying in front of your eyes. I can't really do much for him and I feel terrible about it. But surely I can bring about a change in someone else's life. If I can do that…I will think I saved a part of my brother's happiness somewhere in this world.'

Dhruv couldn't hide his shock. 'I am so sorry, Mithun. I never really knew about your brother; we seldom talk to each other at work.'

Mithun nodded. 'I think almost everybody else knows about it, apart from you.'

In the awkward silence that followed, Dhruv found himself recalling his last conversation with Mithun. He could not recall when they had last spoken like this.

'I can understand how hard it is for you and how much it hurts,' Mithun spoke to break the silence.

'Yes, and I am guilty. I still remember how obviously excited he was that day as we were going to Brahmi soon. The dumbest thing I ever did was to take his car that day and let Aamir walk out of that door to meet Vratika.

'I suppose that he died instantly or the only better probability that he went missing. But if he was alive, I would've got some clue of him being alive. I've looked for him everywhere, including all hospitals and every possible place where he could be. Worst part is, he or I would never know how he died. Was he thinking about his girlfriend Anvi or planning our trip to Brahmi? Was he thinking why Vratika did this to me or was he as smiling and happy as ever?

'The bottom line is he is gone and I have to live all my life without him with a guilt of not being able to find him or with a guilt of not doing my own brother's last rituals. In the worst case, I'll never know what I should be blamed for. This incident has changed my life entirely…forever. I so wish that nobody else goes through the pain that I'm going through right now. I wish I could save my brother's life.'

Mithun hesitated. 'It is an irreparable loss, and it's impossible to find a replacement for such a loss, but life moves on, Dhruv. I think you need to accept change, embrace change and live your life as it comes your way. I know it's much easier said than done, but don't fill your heart with excruciating sadness. This time of darkness, and intense pain too will go gradually pass, and that's the reality. Remember, the rays of hope are always present, even in the darkest hour. That's the only truth. You too need to move on after accepting the fact that Aamir is no more; the earlier, the better. You still have a long way to go. You need to stay strong and positive.'

Dhruv was speechless as he rose and went to get a new bottle of wine. He made another drink for both of them.

Mithun spoke some more about his brother. When his brother was a child, he was told he was special, loved by god and possessing the power to do the right thing and save the world. In his present condition, he often asked for the powers that his family used to talk about. No one could answer his questions or look him in the eye. Mithun spoke in a calm and measured tone, 'People are drinking, smoking, doing drugs and living life like legends, but my brother is too young to even know about all this, Dhruv. He is too innocent to deserve even a part of the pain that he's going through.'

Dhruv acknowledged his point with a heavy nod. Mithun continued, 'He has gone through so much already. The last thing I want for him is to think that he's being a burden on us. I once found him saying this to the doctor. It broke me,' he said, breathing deeply and smiling sadly.

Dhruv was speechless. They both knew there wasn't anything more to say. This conversation was so unexpected and heartbreaking. Mithun's story had shaken Dhruv that night. He felt guilty to imagine that his friend would lose his brother, forever, as he had done.

Mithun's eyes shone with tears and he shut them tight to hold his tears back. He was unable to stop tears pouring from his eyes. 'He's not leaving,' he told himself. They would have all the time in the world soon; there'll be an alternative to make him as perfect as he was. But it wasn't easy. He knew both of his brother's kidneys had failed. They had not noticed the symptoms earlier, and had delayed the dialysis. He wished he could give his life for him, but unfortunately, he couldn't even do that. The world suddenly seemed cruelly unfair to Mithun. How could it happen to his little brother? He reached for a tissue to wipe away his tears, and became his normal self in a little while.

'You're doing a good thing, you know, taking a break. Make it even more useful. Follow Aamir's plan and go to your hometown Brahmi. I am sure it'll bring out change for your own betterment and also lift up your mood. I think it will make your brother happy and give you the chance to see what your past was like.'

'I don't think it's necessary, Mithun.'

'Of course, it is. Stop running away from it. It will help you regain your strength and soon you'll be back at work. '

Dhruv shook his head. 'Who cares about work now anyway?'

'Don't you care about Aamir's wish of going to Brahmi? You just told me how excited he was about this impending trip. Moreover, you can't spend the rest of your life like this, regretting your brother's death. You can't make it conditional.'

'I am not. I should have understood earlier that I've always been an irresponsible, ignorant person and I figure out now that he died because of that very reason.'

'Yes, you are, Dhruv. Stop saying all this. You've tried everything possible after that accident. As I see it, you are clearly on the threshold of great changes in your life. If you keep on living life like this, it will be a great disservice to your brother's memory. After all, he did a great deal to give you a good life while he was alive. Spend some time with nature, help someone, discover something refreshing and learn something from everything that you do there.'

Dhruv had to admit that Mithun's words made him think. He had stood by him when he needed him the most, like an elder brother. Of course both of them were struggling in their own lives, but Mithun was trying his best to make Dhruv believe that they could still live, to do good. After some more talk, Mithun went home and Dhruv thanked him earnestly for coming over. The front door was locked and the house was suddenly quiet, leaving Dhruv alone with his thoughts. Mithun's words kept ringing in his ears, filling him up, as if drawing out his hidden strength.

Dear Rubeena,

I am writing this letter to request a leave for 30 days following the sad and untimely demise of my elder brother Aamir in the recent Mumbai serial blasts. This is a very distressing and testing time for me and I must take further off from 27th July to 16th August. I also request you to please add my recent days of absence to this leave and oblige.

I will be leaving town tomorrow, but you or any of my colleagues can contact me on my personal number if my assistance is required.

I am looking forward to a positive response from you.

Sincerely,

Dhruv

Next morning, his leave got approved via an email that came with a condolence letter. With the office front taken care of, he soon planned to leave for Brahmi.

27 July 2006

It was yet another morning that brought no hope. Clueless, indifferent to the noisy world around him, Dhruv took a cab to the railway station from just outside his apartment. His eyes looked lost, and he stared blankly ahead. It was a ten-minute drive to the station. He took a deep breath and walked to the ticket counter, carrying a backpack over his shoulders. The next train was due in fifteen minutes. He bought the tickets, fiddled inside his pockets to search for money and handed it over with an exasperated sigh. The man at the ticket counter gave him an irritated stare. He left the counter with an apologetic expression on his face and went to the platform.

As he waited for the train on an isolated part of the platform, he replayed the events of the past few days in his mind. He could see himself trying desperately to focus on his work in the office and yet crying for hours in the washroom every day. He tried to maintain his composure and looked around at the other passengers bustling along the railway platform. He felt as if he was looking at them from a different world…from a place far away.

His disruptive thoughts halted suddenly when he found his train waiting for its passengers. He stood up and strode towards it. The last thing he wanted was to run into anyone he knew. He kept his head down and quickly got onto the train without looking around. After taking a secluded seat, he felt he couldn't hold on anymore and wept, tears streaming down his face. He could not help but recall the incident that had taken place two weeks ago. The memory almost paralyzed him. He let the moment pass. After a while, he began to mindlessly check his cell phone, then his bag, to take his mind off its turbulence. The last few days had been mercilessly hard on him. His hands brushed through that photograph. He took it out, gently moved his fingers on its surface, gazed at it for a while and then put it back carefully. He thought, 'No, I can't ever tell anyone. There's not the slightest possibility that I would be understood. They would think of me as the sole culprit. I have to bury it within me and live with it.' The anger, the gloom and the guilt now took the form of a fatal dullness, a life without life. He wondered where it would lead.

A sudden desire to throw up forced him to get up and move to the washroom at the other end of the carriage. He looked at his reflection in the mirror hung above the wash basin. Jerking his head sideways, he splashed cold water on his face, lit a cigarette and smoked while looking out at the trees and clouds outside that swept past his eyes as the train picked up speed. Everything could have been entirely different. If it hadn't been for that day, that moment...how could everything go so utterly wrong? He tried to vent his frustration through the rings of smoke puffing out from his cigarette.

He returned to his seat. He thumbed through an old book from his bag that he'd read hundreds of times already. His reading was disturbed as two preteen boys began to fight over a pair of sunglasses, which evidently belonged to the older brother. After a round of calling each other names, smacking and hitting each other, the older boy gave up the sunglasses to his younger brother saying, 'Alright, you can have them. Just don't break them. Happy?' The younger one hugged his brother with a cry of joy. They played together for a while and then soon fell fast asleep on the same berth.

Dhruv stared at the two of them, snuggled together, sleeping in peace. His emotions resurfaced. All those feelings, the memories, the traumas...it all came back. He shook his head and looked away. After a minute or two, he closed his eyes and dozed off. When he woke up, he found the compartment full of people. Some were busy ordering food, while the others were talking a great deal. Dhruv smiled slightly at the significantly serious comments of people on issues so insignificant to them. Every once in a while, a head would turn up in Dhruv's direction to seek approval for what the person had said, and Dhruv would nod without paying attention to what was being talked about.

'Drop by for a drink some time; we'll have a gala time together.' One passenger said to another. In all the talk, no one seemed to remember the hopes, the dreams and the lives that were crushed some days ago...a day that had become a haunting nightmare for Dhruv; a nightmare that had suffocated him for so long. After making futile attempts to sleep, Dhruv finally took out his phone, put on the earphones and played loud music to distract himself. He was soon in a recurring dream in which he frantically tried to hold on to a string of time and stop it from moving on. He held onto it with all his strength. He became breathless. His facial expression tightened. He breathed heavily and covered his face with his arms.

Dhruv knew that time, unfortunately, didn't heal all pain. He knew that some wounds deepened with time, so that the wounded person could take no more. He was afraid of life, a life which seemed to lead nowhere; lost in the search for any meaningful purpose. He had to walk towards an unknown place.

28 July 2006

It was a beautiful day in Kanhal, known for its unspoilt beauty. Kanhal wasn't a crowded place. He sat in silence at the station for some time and enjoyed the beautiful view around him. He saw little children, laughing and smiling with their friends and relatives. People were filled with the excitement of receiving their loved ones. After a while, he stood up and started walking to an unknown destination rather than taking a cab or bus. He saw a small lake on his way; it wasn't large, but surely much more beautiful than anything he'd ever seen in Mumbai. He saw groups of swans in the distance.

He noticed a dark cloud overhead. Dhruv looked up and was amazed at the sight of thousands of birds flying so close together that he couldn't even see the sky. The birds were flying back home, chirping in ecstasy. It was then that the skies grew dark; there was a sudden thundering, followed by abrupt rain. Although he wanted to soak in the shower, Dhruv hurried on his way.

He took the road north after confirming the route with villagers who advised him to take a bus or a taxi as it was too far. But against their advice, he preferred to move and explore; he just followed the signboards and kept walking. It was the walk that changed his life forever. People waved from their vehicles whenever they saw someone on the street, whether they knew the person or not. He looked around for a place to stay because it was getting cold and the rain showed no signs of stopping soon. He zipped up his jacket against the wind. The trees in the gardens up the hill rustled, as if they were talking. He was dazzled by the scenery; he was certain that the tourists who came here must expect heaven to be as beautiful as Kanhal.

With a sigh, he felt it all coming back to him. He closed his eyes and recalled the years of his childhood. He recalled the days when he was so young and innocent; he recalled the beauty of the farmland and the familiar streets, which had now widened. He recalled those light happy moments, when they were a happy family, a family of four, when he was eight years young.

He kept his eyes tightly shut to recall those days with greater intensity. When he opened his eyes, he realized that little had changed in the last twenty years in Kanhal. It felt as warm as it used to when he was a child. But he was still a few miles away from his destination.

The stars came out as evening turned to night, after the heavy rain. The world was glowing with an eerie blue light. There was complete silence all around. He stood up from the roadside where he had stopped for rest and started walking again. It took greater effort than he thought it would; he was tired, but he kept walking, taking small steps. His legs wobbled; his vision blurred with exhaustion and he struggled to move further with a heavy bag on his shoulder. He knew it was his wish to experience the place by walking, not in a bus. He had already walked some ten kilometres since morning. He sat down once again and spent a few minutes looking at the picture of his family. He thought back to the times they had shared and realized how life had changed drastically in all those years.

He unzipped his bag and took out the flowers his father had given him long ago, according to Aamir. These were now old and faded and tied together with a ribbon, dry and brittle and difficult to handle without breaking. He almost felt as if they represented wishes and blessings from his father.

'Thank you dad,' he whispered, touching the flowers to his closed eyes. He wondered if his father had heard him and he waited for a sign. But there was nothing. He was saddened, for he realized that it had been his brother's wish to return…a wish that could never be granted anymore. He leaned forward and then kissed the picture and the flowers.

This was not how he'd imagined it would end. He'd always assumed his visit to Brahmi would bring some magic into his life.

He missed Aamir. He was his family. Aamir was the only reason for him to live. He couldn't help thinking about the bittersweet memories he shared with his brother. He knew that they would always be together. But life seemed to never stop throwing boulders in his path. Nothing lasts, ever. Every person you'd ever loved leaves you. Every memory you'd ever cherished, leaves you. So do dreams and hopes, until you are left with the sheer desolation of never being able to hope again for anything that's bright.

He continued walking and realized he had walked exactly twelve kilometres since morning when he saw a signboard indicating the route to Brahmi. He slowed his steps and finally stopped to ensure he was on the right path and looked a little higher. He saw another sign board indicating the distance, Brahmi - 3 kms.

He climbed up further into the hills, walking on a narrow stony path with dense forest on both sides. He could hear the movements of animals and night birds from within the forest. He now walked with increased alertness, his hands raised to defend himself.

His mouth went dry and he could feel his body going numb. The sun was about to rise in a couple of hours and he wondered whether he would ever be able to enjoy a sunrise again. He continued to stare at the forest, his eyes missing nothing, remembering the brief time he had spent there with his family. But in all that time, he didn't think of the past – not even once – for he was haunted by visions of his parents struggling for life and of being so helpless.

He kept walking, crumbling.

'Life isn't about stopping; it's a continuous learning process, and whenever you're down, think of the shining sun in all its majesty, all its power, all its grandeur. Don't cry, do not be dismayed.' He remembered his brother's words as he drew nearer to Brahmi. 'My brother loved me more than he loved himself,' he thought.

Dhruv could barely stay upright. He was weak now, though he had managed to walk since morning without food or water. His legs were shaking as if at any moment they would collapse under his weight. The nocturnal noises of the forest were distracting him. He wanted to talk to his brother or his parents, but none of it was real.

Then his thoughts leapfrogged, and he was standing at a crematorium, doing the final rituals for somebody. He couldn't see the face under the logs. It was all blurred as he tried harder to concentrate; he swayed, almost losing his balance, and lurched towards a tree. His breathing became ragged and he started to feel cold, so cold that it almost felt like being frozen to death. He was shivering uncontrollably. Everything was going in and out of focus. He couldn't understand why he had left Brahmi, such a heavenly abode, for Mumbai, where no one would wait or care for him. He couldn't make sense of what was happening; couldn't understand why he was there or why he hated himself with a burning rage. He wanted the shadows of the dark forest to wash over him. He thought perhaps it would all get better when the lights went down and he blacked out.

29 July 2006

Dhruv opened his eyes to a gray morning sky. His breath puffed out in little white clouds. It had been a long and difficult journey; he mused over everything he had seen on his way. When he looked around, it didn't take him long to understand that he'd grown up in a house located close by. Everything felt wonderful and just perfect.

Dhruv had returned to Brahmi, his own home after a twenty-years-long absence. It was just as perfect as Aamir had described to him some days ago – all of it. Aamir's view about their house and Brahmi seconded the present view. He sensed the fairy-tale aura of Brahmi, which drove all thoughts of his present life out of his mind.

For a moment Dhruv felt he'd travelled back in time. His past came rushing back to him in that moment. He could see some houses, different shops, small restaurants and general stores around. One of those was his own property.

He realized that the house looked almost the same to the best of his memories since he'd last visited Brahmi. He gradually noticed the details as he moved closer. It was a very beautiful rural set up of a big two-floored house. The house side walls were standing on bamboo boards. Surprisingly, there was no rust along the roof, no thick layer of moss in the backyard and no walls were dripping with greasy water. His house had beautiful traditional sliding windows with balustrade windows to his view and everything outside the house looked just perfect and well-cared for. The bricks used gave an elegant view and Dhruv could imagine how marvellous the view would be in the past years.

Dhruv closed his eyes, as if to return to the thoughts of what the house had once been – an image of perfect splendour and simplicity. Despite all that had happened in the last few days, he was glad to be there once again. The brief period when he had lived there flashed before his eyes. It seemed incredible and unbelievable to him.

The house had been built some hundred years ago; it was his forefathers' home, making it one of the oldest in the area. He walked through the house for the next few minutes, noticing how good it looked, despite the ravages of time. It looked like it was decently taken care of by somebody in all these years. It was huge, and the basic structure stood tough against the test of time. He made mental notes of all that he had to do to bring his home back to life. He realized the task would be arduous, for there was much work that needed to be done. He was relieved that he had found a purpose to live for.

When he looked out, he saw a girl seated at the window of the neighbouring house; their eyes met for a second. He felt himself twitch as he remembered Vratika and looked away.

A dog barked in the distance and Dhruv realized he had been standing with the front door open for quite a long time. He quickly closed it. Walking inside, he saw an old man sitting there.

'Hey, you, boy…come here!' he called out authoritatively. Dhruv said nothing; he stared as the old man called out to him from the backyard. For a while, he wasn't sure whether he should go.

The old man was sitting on a wooden bench, holding a kulhad filled with steaming tea. His face was wrinkled, but he still had a powerful voice. He gave Dhruv an unblinking stare. Dhruv walked up to him. In the few minutes that Dhruv had been there, no one in the village had accosted him for any reason. He wondered who that man was, what he wanted, and what was he doing in his house.

'I have never really seen you here before; it seems like you're new.'

'This used to be my home. I have returned here after twenty years. Who are you and what are you doing here?'

'I am the caretaker of this place. Mr. Das appointed me. You must be knowing him if you own this house,' he said.

'Not really. As I said, It's been a while that I've been here.'

The old man closed the door of the house and directed him to move towards Mr. Das's house which was just five minutes away. When they reached and the caretaker narrated his sudden arrival, Mr. Das asked him, 'Who are you?'

'I am Dhruv. My parents used to live here in this house. They were killed by a tiger in the woods twenty years ago. My brother Aamir and I left soon afterwards. I have come back for a short visit. That home still remains with us.'

The old man suddenly rose to his feet in surprise and hugged Dhruv. 'Oh, God. The world is indeed a small place. How could I have imagined I'd meet you again.' Dhruv was baffled.

The old man, or Mr. Das as he was called by the villagers, who was now a teacher at the nearby school in Kanhal was his father's close friend. He and Dhruv's father had set up a farming business like many others in the village, but they had opened a general store along with it too.

'I always asked your father to move our business out and expand it, but he was adamant about never leaving Brahmi. It was his dream to watch it grow and flourish. Your father was a man of vision, Dhruv. Oh, you might not remember much. You were very young, and since then, I have been in touch with Aamir only. I don't think Aamir ever discussed anything about me with you. Anyway, where is Aamir? Though it's been quite long that we met, we still talk over phone sometimes. He will recognize me in a moment. Has he come too?'

Dhruv was teary-eyed at the mention of his brother's name, and told Mr. Das all about the attack in which he had lost Aamir forever. Mr. Das was shocked and sad.

'I can't believe my ears. Aamir was a brilliant boy. Yes, he was. I spoke to him a month back only. He said he was planning a trip here with you. I clearly remember how I met Aamir after your parent's death and suggested him to go to Mumbai as he didn't want to stay here anymore. I asked him to wait for some days and connected him to some people there who would take care of both of you and your education. My college friend Vijay was settled in Mumbai and he took good care of both of you for some years. I occasionally dropped by to check if both of you were doing fine and the frequency of my visits decreased once Aamir started taking evening classes for college and started working in day time and got busy with that.'

He took a pause.

'So, this is why you are here now. The doors of Brahmi are always open to you, son. You can start some work and live here.' Mr. Das patted Dhruv's shoulders sympathetically.

'No, uncle. I will have to resume my life in Mumbai. I am working there and I've got certain duties to fulfil.'

'Oh, yes. Mumbai never fails to enchant people, especially the young, with all its noise, speed and flashy lights. But mark my words boy, the things you want to go to Mumbai for will one day send you back here, because this is your real home. You feel alive here. I speak from personal experience,' Mr. Das spoke, gazing into the distance.

Dhruv learnt that Mr. Das was a well educated man. He held a doctorate degree in English and had studied in Mumbai. Those were the days when a telephone was a luxury only the rich could afford. When Mr. Das returned to his village, he learned that his father had passed away a month ago and his family faced financial ruin. It was Dhruv's father who supported him through the roughest phase of his life and helped his family get back on their feet.

Dhruv shared his thoughts and story with the old man. Dhruv was in two minds about staying on in Brahmi for the rest of his life. He felt his mind and soul would be somewhat restored in the few days that he would spend there. Brahmi had started working its magic the moment he stepped onto its soil. But he knew he ought to go back to Mumbai. Aamir had wanted a different life for him; he owed it to his brother to live up to his expectations and not hide away in Brahmi. He had to face the real world out there.

Mr. Das stared at him with tears pouring down his face. It was evident that he was at a loss for words. Mr. Das got him to his feet, took him into the kitchen and prepared a cup of tea from herbs and tea grown in Brahmi. He did not raise the subject that they had been discussing, so he began to speak of something else till Dhruv interrupted him.

'You knew my father better than anybody else. Tell me about him. I want to know.'

'I can't imagine anyone forgetting about him, he was such a wonderful person. It was strange how time played tricks, and changed our lives forever. I was there and I was unable to save him. I was so shaken that I couldn't go to work for several days after that. I could hear or see nothing around me; all I heard was the sound of my own voice when I wept. What kind of a friend was I to not be able to do anything to make both of you happier!'

Dhruv thought of the life he might have lived here had they never left Brahmi. He couldn't imagine it. 'How did my father spend his days here?'

Mr. Das spoke, 'Your father was a disciplined man who rose at dawn. He was very devout and went to the temple every day.'

Brahmi is an ancient place and such were the beliefs of people here which are lost in the run of time somewhere. After the attacks, many communities left Brahmi and shifted their base to Kanhal.

Mr. Das had listened to him as he'd briefly described how Aamir and he had lived in Mumbai, and how the police informed him about Aamir's death in a terrorist attack. It was evident that Mr. Das felt a certain stab of guilt for not being there for his friend's children. Now, he wanted to do everything possible to keep Dhruv happy and offered him to stay at his house.

For the first time since they'd met, there were unexplained tears in Dhruv's eyes. 'Thank you so much for telling me all this. Aamir had given me a glimpse into it, but hearing it from you has connected all the dots for me. Had you not looked after our house, I wouldn't have known about you and my father. Thank you for being so nice to me and offering me to stay here. That's the greatest thing in the world that anyone could have offered to me right now. But I would like to stay at my house for some days and relive all those moments yet again.' Dhruv was deeply moved to see the regard in which Mr. Das held his parents so many years after their death.

'I did only what your father would have done for anybody else had he been still alive,' Mr. Das replied humbly. In the silence that followed, Dhruv suddenly realized how lucky he was to have met his father's childhood friend and know more about their life.

'I shall take your leave now.' Dhruv said.

'Wait,' Mr. Das said. He walked to his bedroom and returned with a big packet, which he gave to Dhruv.

'What's in it?' he asked.

'It's your father's share of the store that we used to run years ago. I think I would justify our friendship if I give it to you.'

'I'm really sorry but I can't accept it,' Dhruv said.

'I really want you to take it. I can't keep your share with me. It will enable you to live a better life in the future. Had your father or Aamir lived, I would've handed it over to them. Now that they are no longer there, I think you deserve this.' Dhruv watched him closely as he spoke.

'I want to thank you for such a kind gesture. I haven't really spent much time with my family and I don't remember much of my childhood either, but I am sure if he was alive, he would've behaved much as you have. It almost feels as if I am standing before my own father.'

'It's the least I could do. I just did what anyone who knew your parents would have done. I think your parents did the best they could for you. And your upbringing has a lot to do with it. This never-give-up attitude...your parents were winners. They won many hearts.'

Dhruv smiled. He changed his mind and stayed a little longer at Mr. Das's house. They spent the day talking of his parents, his occasional visits at their home as caretaker from a couple of decades, his forefathers and Aamir. Mr. Das did the best he could to make Dhruv feel at home, although he felt he had not done enough. Dhruv left Mr. Das's house at sundown, bidding the older man farewell, and returned home with the promise to visit him again sooner before leaving Brahmi. He watched the branches of trees waving in the wind, preparing him for the rain tonight.

As he walked, he replayed the events of the day in his mind, thinking not only about his family, but also about Mr. Das, who had been so kind to him. Like him, Mr. Das had no family left in the world, which was why he wanted Dhruv to return to Brahmi. It was the first time he had ever spoken to someone other than Aamir about his father.

A little later, he thought of how his life would change on his return to Brahmi. Consciously or unconsciously, he'd been leading a life in the last few days that would prove him to be a better and more mature person.

And as he walked, he wondered how long he had been away from Brahmi and whether his extended family would come to visit him at least once.

'What would it be like to have my family by my side forever now?' he wondered.

Lightning tore through the sky outside that night. It seemed his childhood was back in a flash, now that he had returned to Brahmi, to the lap of nature. There was an exotic beauty the next morning; the air was crisp, fresh and chilly. As he walked by the other house, the girl he had seen earlier was standing by the wooden fence, watching the sky as if to enjoy the exquisiteness of the morning. From the window, he saw the broken-down house.

Trees were toppling nearby and roofs were tearing off. Something that could make the house more vulnerable was flying past. As he entered his home, he saw a photograph hung on the wall. It was taken on his mother's birthday, he recalled. His two-floored spacious house evidenced by beautiful coconut trees indicated how prominent they were. Those long pillars lying at every ten feet seemed to be made of 'iron-wood'. His home was very beautifully architecturally designed.

He remembered how Aamir and he used to run across the house and sit in the balcony here, mimicking their father reading the newspaper. It brought back every single memory in just a few seconds. He was looking intently at the wooden chair placed in the corner of a room where his dad used to sit. He'd known that he would be the only person in the house, but what he hadn't realized was how it would shatter him to be alone in a home haunted by the echoes of the past.

But sitting there in silence, he became more certain with every passing moment that he wanted to spend more time in Brahmi. He struggled with the dark secret that still overshadowed him. He was lonely, with nothing much to do. He decided to clean the house, treasure everything that was within and make it as lively as he could for himself. Make it livelier as he would spend the next few days there, to relive the past. The essence was the only thing he could resurrect by bringing a few things back to their old shape and place.

❀

The sun had set a few hours ago and it was a bitterly cold evening in Brahmi. The sky was dark, and the wind cut through him like a knife as he stepped out of the house after a tiring day to sit on the wooden chair in the veranda. His expression was a mixture of tiredness, sadness and patience. He wished that his family was there at this moment. It was catastrophic for him to wait for something he knew would never happen; but he just couldn't give up because it was everything that he had ever wanted.

It had taken him twenty years to return to Brahmi. He recalled the memories of the childhood he'd shared with Aamir. He'd been constantly thinking about his earlier years in Brahmi since morning. But he knew his journey wasn't over yet. Life was a winding road; he had somehow circled back to the place where he belonged.

The moon had risen and the air had cooled slightly as Dhruv started walking around to see the place. The sky was getting darker with every passing moment. All he knew was that he'd be here for some days and needed to purchase things of necessity. As he walked, he watched everything carefully and was amazed by the soothing silence and peace around. Even though he was tired after walking almost fifteen kilometres that day, he still wanted to see more of Brahmi.

He saw a small restaurant and stood there for a minute without saying anything to anybody working there. It was the second time he had crossed that restaurant that day.

The restaurant owner was sitting outside on a chair, and said jovially, 'You don't have to think too much before having food. It isn't that bad.'

'What do you mean?' he asked.

'Well, it looks like you're hungry and this time is just right to have dinner.' He grinned.

'Yes, of course. Thanks,' he smiled and said.

'Come inside. Will serve you the best of the vegetarian food we have.' He winked and ordered food for Dhruv. 'You look new here?'

'Yes…kind of.'

'Are you a writer or filmmaker who is in search of a beautiful non-destroyed place? I have seen many such seekers land up in Brahmi,' the owner said and grinned again.

'Not really. I was born here and have come back after many years. It's a short visit. My parents died quite long back here and we left the place then. I am just here to spend some beautiful time.' He said, signalling towards his house, which was visible from the restaurant. He had said this lightly, but within him, he knew well that this wasn't exactly the reason why was here.

As if knowing exactly what to do, the owner smiled sympathetically. He thought, perhaps by talking about something else, anything else, he'd be able to relax him.

'So, you know anybody around here?' he asked.

'Yes, I've just met Mr. Das this morning; he was my father's friend. I'm not sure if you know him.'

'Of course I know him. In fact, everybody knows each other here. It's a small place…like an island where you know everything about each other and you know you've to live your life just around these people,' he said happily.

Food was served. It took Dhruv a second to register it, but as soon as he started having his meal, he realised how much he loved it. It took him ten minutes to finish the food, while the restaurant owner narrated some beautiful stories about Brahmi.

The restaurant owner stretched his arms out, yawned and said, 'Do you need something to drink?'

Checking his watch, he saw that it would be dark soon and he wouldn't mind drinking after sometime.

'Yes, I wouldn't mind a whisky.'

Giving him a bottle, he said, 'We just have this one left, if that's fine with you.'

'Yes, it's perfectly fine and thanks for the lovely food and beautiful stories you told me about Brahmi.'

'Aha! Don't mention. You can drop in anytime for delicious food and beautiful stories. I'll be more than happy to be at your service again.'

'I'd like that,' he said and made a mental note of coming to this restaurant again. He left for a brief evening walk before he was finally ready to take a drink that night.

He poured a glass of whiskey for himself and glanced into the adjacent house, trying to check whether the girl was still there. Neither of them moved as they faced each other. Though they were quite close, he didn't speak to her. He didn't recognize her. He had thought it would be easier somehow if she knew what to say. But she didn't. Everything that came into his head seemed inappropriate and lacking.

She looked attractive, Dhruv thought as he looked at her. He shook his head, looked down into his glass and felt embarrassed for staring at her like that. He just hoped that she didn't think he was crazy. When he looked up again, the girl was gone.

'Excuse me,' said a voice at Dhruv's door, 'I have never seen you here before.' Dhruv was startled. He hadn't expected her to be so quick. In fact, he thought she would be offended by his inappropriate staring.

Dhruv watched her walk in, noticing again how beautiful she was. After meeting Vratika, he'd always been less interested in appearance and beauty than in the unseen traits: kindness and integrity, humour and sensibility.

'Yes,' he replied.

'Sorry, but I've never seen you here before. In fact, this house has been empty for the past few years that I have lived here,' she said, sounding suspicious.

'My roots are in this village. For the past twenty years, nobody lived here. My parents died in an accident long back and we moved to Mumbai after that. But now, this is where I am supposed to be.' He paused. 'But what about you?' he asked softly, suspecting he'd receive a weird response.

It was a long moment before she answered.

'I'm a writer. I often come to the house next door about once in a year. It is a beautiful place to explore, and do fresh write-ups. I enjoy being here. It's a nice break from my life in the city. Plus I was brought up here by my grandparents.'

She asked for permission to sit near him; he nodded and she went on.

'Ok great. For how many years have you been coming here?' he asked.

'It's been five years now and I'm fortunate to have lived here at a certain point of my life.'

'So am I.'

He had to admit, it was good to talk to someone who didn't know him. During the past few months, he'd alternated between spending time alone or fending off questions as to whether or not he was feeling okay. More than once, colleagues had recommended the name of a good therapist and confided that the person had helped them or somebody they knew. Dhruv had been tired of giving explanations and receiving sympathy from everybody. And he was even more tired of their concerned glances.

They were silent and they stayed like that for a long time before she finally looked at him and asked, 'So what have you been up to? I hope I am not being impertinent.'

'It's okay. It's good to have a conversation.' He said, smiling, 'I work with a media group in Mumbai and I do marketing for them.'

'That's great! You can help me meet your editor sometime for my write-ups then.'

'Yes, why not!'

'Thank you. I'm so glad we are talking.'

He smiled, but felt his stomach clench when he thought about his brother's death.

'Why are you suddenly here in Brahmi? Is it just a holiday or something?' she said glancing at her hand; he noticed she wasn't wearing a ring.

'No, I had some pending work. I wanted to come here at least once, to see if everything was alright here.' He looked down when he said it, suddenly feeling a little weaker. That's what he was avoiding.

She nodded without expressing surprise. She thought she heard something in his tone, and the next question came automatically.

'Is there anything you want to talk about? I am a stranger; you can trust me. I'm unlikely to share anything you say with anyone you know.'

He didn't answer immediately, as if someone had offered to listen to him for the first time since Aamir's death. He had needed, more than anything, to talk to somebody; to spill out the tight, apprehensive neurotic tensions that crippled his mind. But he just couldn't find an appropriate confidant other than the silence of the night. Not until this girl walked into his house. It was her eyes, he thought, that convinced him to speak.

'What's your name?'

'Sachi.'

'Sachi, unlike my father and brother, I've always been the one who was selfish and created problems for everyone by not respecting some relations, and by over-respecting others.' He paused. 'Do you know about the terrorist attacks on the Mumbai local trains?'

'Yes, I heard of them some days ago. It was terrible.'

'I lost my brother Aamir in that attack.'

He looked at her. She was sitting still with her eyes wide open as if experiencing the unsaid. Dhruv's heart grew tight with the thought of having lost his entire family - earlier his parents, and now his brother in that unfortunate incident.

'I am sorry to have even asked you this question. But I think you wanted to talk about it with somebody after this incident. Consider me that person. I do understand.'

'I shared a lot of memories with him, Sachi. It was Aamir's wish to be here, to celebrate our parents' anniversary here. I am the one responsible for everything that happened.'

The world around Dhruv was growing faint and distant as he said this, as if viewed through the far end of a telescope. He heard the trees swaying back and forth. But instead of a breeze, all he felt was the heat and the humidity. There was nothing left to drink and he was getting tired after a long day at repairing the house. He realized he'd spoken to a stranger, but couldn't remember how it happened. He wanted so much to sleep, to rest for a while.

She shook her head. 'I don't know…' She hesitated, but couldn't complete what she had to say.

'That hurts. But again, you're in no position to talk right now. You should be resting.' Her reply came almost too quickly this time.

His mind raced frantically as he recalled his last conversation with the police; his head spinning as he recalled various moments shared with Aamir. He needed to rest. He couldn't stay awake and his eyes began to close.

As he got up in the middle of the night, he took out an ink pen and tore a page from an old notebook lying in one of the drawers. He sat on his dad's wooden chair and started writing something, with tears filling his eyes. He wrote down all that he had felt since Aamir's accident, made a paper plane out of it and watched it fly somewhere far up above. Dhruv watched it travel across the distance with eyes wide open, assuming it would deliver his message to Aamir; this was no longer the childhood game they had played so long ago.

Aamir,

I want to tell you how I feel about all that has happened, and how I feel about not talking to you for the one last time in my life.

I've been thinking about you constantly since 11th July. I can't even begin to count how many times I've cried or prayed for you to come back. It happened when I least expected it. Had I known it would occur, I would never have agreed to let you travel to Dadar that day. But that does not free me of guilt, of the sin that I committed and let my own brother die. The only person who cared for me the most in the world and never let me feel the absence of mom and dad. Now that I realize you were right about everything that you had said, I also realize that I was wrong, very wrong to ignore what was real and I am dying of guilt now. I've made countless mistakes in my life; sending you to meet Vratika that day being the worst of them all. I was wrong to have acted as I did when you stopped me from getting drunk, advising me to be careful in my relationship with Vratika. I tried to deny the things you were saying, even though I knew they were all true.

Brother, I realize that I don't even know how I am supposed to live my life without you. After all, we were supposed to be here this week. You cared the most for me. Now, you can't fulfil your last wish in this world. Though I know you are the most bighearted person in my life, I doubt if my sin deserves to be forgiven. I'm still trying to make sense of what I feel myself.

I miss you, my brother. But today is especially hard because I am sitting in our home in Brahmi, which reminds me of you, mom and dad and how long you struggled to make everything work out for us both while you were here and how easy you made it look. I am trying to live, though. At night when I am alone, I call for you but you never answer, so I know you're angry with me. I am here because you wanted us to celebrate our parents' anniversary here and also because there is no other place for me to be. I feel my eyes drowning in tears because I know this time you'll never come back. I feel your sadness and my own loneliness. You never complained about my attitude, and always stood by me.

For the first few days after you left, I wanted to believe that I could go on as I always had, without mom and dad. But I couldn't. Every time I sat on the balcony, I could only think of you, brother, and the time that we spent together. But I knew that you would never come back to see me, take care of me, hug me and to tell me what's right or wrong. I wish I could meet you, mom and dad. May be I am too late now. But once in my life, I wish I could for one last time talk to you and tell you how much I love you and want you to come back and hug me. Forgive me please.

Dhruv

30 July 2006

Dhruv woke up when the first rays of the sun shone through the window. He got up and stood in the doorway, looking out. Everything looked green and fresh, and he suddenly felt happy, almost joyful. He left the door open to get the dampness out of the home, stepped outside and started to walk with no idea where he was headed. He soon found himself on a little paved path that led to a small lake nearby where his father used to take him when he was a child. He could remember the two of them walking around the lake, as he listened to his dad's stories and held a basket to keep the useful things they'd pick up on their walk.

He stood lost in thought at the edge of the lake. The rays of the rising sun slanted between the trees, lighting with bars of gold the crystal clear waters of the lake. The splendid view around him reminded him of Sachi. He could visualize her beauty, elegance and piety. She seemed to be the same age as him. Dhruv remembered how patiently she'd listened to every word he had spoken last night. He made a mental note to thank her later that day. His thoughts then moved to his memories of his parents. He imagined them, standing there by the lake, holding hands.

'It's so beautiful and quiet here, isn't it?' Dhruv came out of his trance and turned around. He saw Sachi standing there, smiling at the view of the lake.

'Oh, I didn't notice you here. How long have you been standing here?' Dhruv was startled and spoke hurriedly. He gave a small laugh and said, 'Yeah, totally. It's beautiful here. It soothes my mind.'

'Not too long. I came here a few minutes ago. I didn't want to disturb you.' Sachi didn't take her eyes off the lake.

'I wanted to thank you for last night…for listening, I mean. And, apologize too. I was just…'

'Hey, hold on! You don't have to explain. I understand it all. It's all going to be fine soon.'

Dhruv raised his eyebrow and said half-smilingly, 'Hope so. Anyway, what about you? So you are a writer, right? Mind sharing more on that?'

'Well, I freelance for a travel magazine and write novels. I travel a lot but not like everywhere around. I select places like Brahmi – full of serenity, innocence and beauty. You can feel love and liveliness here each moment.'

'You sound like someone who's deeply in love with somebody,' he said and they both laughed.

'Why, yes, I don't have many people left in my life. I too lost my parents in my childhood, but I've always had enough people for whom I want to live. There's always that somebody for whom one wants to live.'

He looked at her. 'Are you speaking of your personal experience or telling me what you think I need to hear?'

Sachi cleared her throat. 'Well, we are never alone. There are people who have endured experiences similar to ours, and survived; so can we. The universe is full of such stories. No one wants you to give up on this life. Not tonight. Not tomorrow. Not ever.'

Dhruv stood there, staring at her, trying to absorb what she had said. It felt good. It felt empowering. They spent a few more minutes by the lake and then walked back together in silence.

'Well', she said as she crossed her arms, 'I've probably taken enough of your time. I would excuse you if you want.'

'It's okay,' he said, and felt sweat beading on his forehead. 'I would love to spend some more time with you, if you don't mind. I've got nobody here and I'll be bored to death being alone.'

She laughed. 'You sound like you've never been alone before.'

He shrugged. 'I haven't. I've always had my friends or Aamir with me. So, I never actually was so alone.'

'Alright, I'll call you over for a drink this evening then, as I've got to finish a few write-ups. I shall take your leave now.'

He nodded, and watched as she walked on the pebbled trail. He sat on a big stone and looked around him.

He saw cumulus clouds in the sky, and birds chirping merrily in the trees. Since the weather in Brahmi was so unpredictable, he thought of quickly picking up some necessities for the evening and getting home quickly. On the way back, as he walked through the forest, the memories of his parents' deaths in the forest flashed before his eyes. They had come to spend a day picnicking in the forest. Everything was fine, till a tiger leaped on them from behind the bushes. It was horrifying. Dhruv's parents gave themselves up to save their children. He could still hear their cries of sheer agony for Dhruv and Aamir to run away, even as the tiger clawed at them. These memories had traumatized Dhruv for years.

As Dhruv grew up, he felt a terrible emptiness in his soul. He often kept searching for his parents' faces in the crowds wherever he went, and was doing it for Aamir now. He knew it was impossible to see them, but he couldn't help himself. His search was a never-ending quest that was doomed to fail. He wept often, knowing that his parents had been irreplaceable.

In the evening, Dhruv opened the door and sat on the wooden chair in the veranda with a bottle of wine that he had got from the only wine shop half a kilometre away. The veranda wasn't really spacious, but there was sufficient space for two people to sit for a long time and talk their hearts out. He called Sachi and she joined him a few minutes later. He went inside to get some food, and while he was away, she arranged the table and saw a diary in which Dhruv had made some equations with 'Aamir, police, helpline and hospital' written on it. It was hard for her to understand anything out of it. He came back with food on a couple of plates and handed one to Sachi. They talked a while about how they had spent their day, as they shared their meal.

'Seems like you had a really pleasant day.'

'I did.' He looked away from her intent gaze and focused on the swaying trees outside. After a moment, he added, almost to himself, 'One of the best in the last few days.'

'Dhruv, are you OK?' She was staring at him with a mixture of concern and curiosity.

'I'm fine. I was just remembering something I have to take care of.' Dhruv improvised. 'Anyway,' he said, straightening and folding his hands over one raised knee. 'Enough about me. If you don't mind, tell me something moré about yourself. '

Puzzled about what he wanted to know, she started from the beginning, touching on all the basic facts in a little more detail – her job, her upbringing, her hobbies and her parents' accident. Mostly, though, she talked about Rahil, her boyfriend. She described him as a wonderful man and she regretted her inability to spend more time with him.

Dhruv listened as she spoke, not saying much. When she finished, he asked, 'Why don't you spend more time with Rahil, if you're in a relationship with him?'

She felt her chest constrict as if she were suffocating. 'He's gone, Dhruv. He died some time ago due to an unfortunate fatal disease.'

It was then that his breathing suddenly became difficult. His hands began to shake; his body began to tremble.

'I'm so sorry.'

Sachi stared up at him silently. Then, with a single deliberate motion, she wiped away the tears with the back of her hand and said. 'That's OK, Dhruv. I don't want to trade the special moments for tears all my life. It would demean our love. He had been special to me and will always be. I feel him near me whenever I need him the most. Trust me, the people we love the most never actually leave us.'

In the pale glow of the light shining on their table, Dhruv got up from his chair and put a hand on her shoulder supportively. 'I understand how it feels,' he said and then walked to the kitchen to get some more wine.

The stars were glittering like tiny spangles on a magician's cape and the air was moist and cold. As they sat at the table,

Dhruv told Sachi everything about his life and why he felt that he could have saved his brother by the time he finished his drink. Although his vision was bleary by then, he saw Sachi's face fill with light, though he knew it was just his imagination. When she offered the saddest of smiles to console him, he tried hard to hold back the tears, but couldn't.

'You didn't do anything, Dhruv. It wasn't your fault. And well, facts remain the same that it was just an unlucky coincidence and you couldn't do much about it.'

'I know it wasn't my fault, but my heart goes off by the fact that I couldn't even perform the last rituals for my brother,' he said quietly. He couldn't meet her eyes. He was swaying as he got up. Sachi reached for his hand to get him into his bedroom. He cursed himself, knowing he should have been more careful that night as he was unnecessarily causing trouble for Sachi. She helped him get to bed, dimmed the lantern and walked out quietly, leaving Dhruv in silence. With the cold, exhaustion and wine beginning to numb his senses, he fell into deep sleep thereafter.

31 July 2006

Last night, the wind-driven rain poured from the dark skies over Brahmi, streaming down the windows of Dhruv's home. He had woken early that morning and remained awake because he had not eaten much. The eastern horizon was faintly gold in colour. The birds were chirruping and singing. He seized a glass of water from the wooden table and downed it in one gulp, thinking over his behaviour last night. He felt he'd been too afraid of everything. He felt he detested himself.

He walked to the door, and glanced outside. Shafts of sunlight were filtering through the trees into the area surrounding his home, lighting up the wet plants and shrubs. Spider webs glittered like necklaces. A soft mist curled along the ground near the trees, playing along the dark edges. Dhruv stepped out, barefoot on the grass. The ground was wet and cold under his feet. The air smelled fresh. Everything around him was flourishing, healthy and rooted. He kept walking, unaware of his route, till he reached the foot of a hill. Without a thought, he started going uphill. The temperature began to plummet sharply as he reached the summit.

He saw the restaurant owner coming back on the way. 'Hey, good morning. It seems like you're done walking and going back,' Dhruv said, smiling.

'Yes. I wake up at 4'0 clock, then I come here running, exercise for an hour-and-a-half and go back.'

'It sounds like a lot of exercise.'

'Trust me, not much. When I was young like you, I used to work out for three straight hours and even then go for a lot of physical sports in the evening.'

'I won't be able to do even half of your workout.'

'There will always be a difference between urban and rural workout, if you know what I mean,' he said, smilingly and started running as he waved off to Dhruv. He smiled and waved back.

After he got to the top, he was surprised to find Sachi there. The steady rhythm of his footfalls set her mind adrift and she smiled at Dhruv as he drew closer to her. He smiled back, not knowing what to say. 'It's quite a coincidence to find you wherever I go the first thing in the morning.'

'Congratulations! Not everybody is that lucky.' She smiled again.

'Um, yeah, I guess,' he replied in a rather puzzled tone.

She had to admit that Dhruv's story made her feel tense. Not only because of the manner in which Aamir had died, but also because he held himself responsible for his brother's death. It also had to do with the sad way he smiled sometimes, the expression on his face when he'd told her about Aamir and his parents, or the way he was treating himself then. There was a void within him that he couldn't disguise and she knew that it matched her own in some way.

'You were quite unsettled last night. You seemed to be making it all the more hard for yourself and you need to stop thinking so much about it.'

'It seems like every time I talk to you, I end up only talking about that accident. Probably yes, I have to stop thinking too much about it and respect the life my brother has given me.'

She picked up a stone and threw it as far as she could and said, 'Yes. I don't want you to think that you can't talk about anything else and that all you can do is live in the past.'

He remained silent for the next few minutes.

'Do you need some help?' she asked.

He shook his head. 'I can handle this. I know what to do.'

'You loved him very much, didn't you?'

'Yes,' he answered.

'He was your only family. He was more than a brother. He was your mother and father too. Right?'

'Yes.'

'Then which parents in the world would feel glad about their son crying and feeling sad out of sheer guilt in an unsuccessful attempt to save his brother? You should talk about him with pride for the beautiful moments you shared, and the life he gave you after so many struggles. He gave up his entire life to make yours happy. You just can't afford to let his effort go in vain like this.'

Dhruv remained silent, and Sachi took it as a cue to continue further.

'Sometimes we have to let go of what is killing us. What is coming will come and we will meet it when it does. You have to stop being so pathetic and gloomy all the time. Do you really think your heart shattering and tear jerking letter to your brother would delight him? He deserves peace now and you are not helping him at all by being so miserable. For a change, try sending a letter that talks of the good times you've shared; something which you don't regret. I think you'll get your answers, the reply you are waiting for.'

'I doubt that. You're just saying that to make me happy.'

She shrugged, leaving it open to interpretation. 'Why would I do that?'

'I don't know...but you're saying it to make me happy.'

'You can't let your life pass by just like that, Dhruv. You can't be this hopeless. Good and evil co-exist in this world, and all this works together in your life. How you react to it shows your own purpose of life. It's a mystery, but the only way you're going to find out if there's something bright and better waiting for you out there is by first *believing* that there is something brighter and better out there. It may sound bizarre but sometimes something so small, like this tiny flower or a blade of grass can keep you alive. Think about it. You've got to find something worth living for. You deserve it.'

She studied him standing lost in thoughts for a while. 'Fair enough,' she finally broke the silence again, 'So anyway, as you already magically knew this, let me show you something that you've failed to notice.' She pointed out to an engraved stone there, the very stone that both the brothers had seen growing up. The sight of it made him smile, and Sachi, seeing him smile, smiled back and moved to the stone where the engraved letters said - *Aamir and Dhruv. Best friends and brothers forever.*

It brought back all the good memories of his childhood and he couldn't help but stare at it for many minutes. But that life was gone now, he reminded himself. These were extraordinary events in his present painful life. The concept felt alien now but it left him feeling strangely elated and motivated at exactly the same time.

'My heart is still broken, but I will never quit smiling. I cherish every minute of the twenty-five years I got to spend with Aamir. I'll honour him by taking care of myself from now on.' Dhruv looked at her, as if to thank her. She gave him the most reassuring smile.

'Let's go,' she said and they started on the way back. Dhruv remained silent till they had climbed off the hill. He kept fighting his thoughts till he was able to believe that life was the way Sachi had described, and not the way he thought it to be, since Aamir died. Thanking Sachi, he reached home and wrote yet another letter.

Aamir,

I write this letter under a beautiful light as you lie sleeping in some other world. Twenty days have passed since I heard from you last and talked to you. Losing our parents was hard enough; to have lost you as well was a shock to me. I realized the special bond that we shared since childhood when Sachi showed me that engraved stone today. It was almost like you being on my side again, though I know that my life would never be the same. I want you back, more than I ever wanted anything. I was a fool to not spend most of my time with you, and I've come to realize that you were the most important thing that I will ever have in this world.

I remember coming back to Brahmi the other day and meeting Sachi for the first time. I was so afraid and filled with guilt after your death, because I was so certain that you would never forgive me for having done this to you. I was shaking as I heard about your death from the police and almost held myself responsible for it. When I was depressed and sad, I forgot for a moment how you struggled to give me this life, make me stand where I am today and gave me memories to cherish for a lifetime. But Sachi explained to me the worth of your effort again, which I shouldn't have forgotten at all. How can I ever imagine that somebody who jumped off the mountains just to make me happy can really be angry with me for anything in this world? In all our years together, you never really left a stone unturned to see me happy, nor did you question me when I spent almost all your savings on my luxuries. And when I came in with tears in my eyes, you always knew whether I needed you to hold me or to just let me be. I don't know how you knew but you did, and you made it easier for me.

Brother, I love you and I always will. I was wrong to have acted as I did in the past few days. Sachi was right about everything. You have inspired and supported me all my life. You'll never know how much it has meant to me. Not everyone can claim on doing and sacrificing things the way you did for us. It surely takes a man with a heart to do that. And you did that for twenty years. You're my best friend and my brother, and I treasure all our memories now.

You are the most forgiving and gentle person I know. God is with you, he must be, for you are the closest thing to an angel that I've ever met.

Now when I try to remember the way we once were, I realize I love you so deeply that I'll find ways to come back to you despite your not being in this world. It is my deepest wish that you give me one more chance in life and I'll make you proud. I promise you that. Now, with my gaze fixed toward the future, I see your face and hear your voice, certain that this is the path I must follow, I'll put all my efforts to reach the love of your life, to make sure that she's doing okay without you. I promise I'll always be there with her as a younger brother.

I hope this letter reaches you wherever you are. I hope I receive your reply to it, no matter its shape and form. I need your blessings and your love. I love you brother and I am so sorry for not telling you when I should have. Know that I loved you, I love you, and I always will.

This isn't goodbye, Aamir. I express my thanks to you through this note. Thank you for being the greatest part of my life and giving me joy, for loving me, for caring for me when I needed it the most, for never making me miss our parents and for making me a proud brother. Thank you for all the memories that I will cherish forever. But most of all, thank you for getting me back to my roots; this magical place called Brahmi and reacquainting me with my childhood here. I am here to celebrate our parents' anniversary tomorrow and receive all your love in return. Be with me. I am happy!

Dhruv

1 August 2006

Standing in the veranda, Dhruv wrapped his hands around the coffee cup to warm them as he stared into the adjacent home to look for Sachi. Although he wished that Aamir was around, he also wanted to think positive and celebrate his parents' anniversary. Despite the sorrow he had endured recently, he'd spent the past night recalling family vacations and blissful days when they had been content with the world. His parents' wedding photograph, which depicted both of them smiling, was prominently displayed in the room.

He reached for the picture on the wall and started saying what was in his heart.

'We know the reason why I am here. Although they say that you don't really appreciate your parents until you become one, I don't agree. There's so much more to say on the occasion of your anniversary. We have greatly appreciated both of you, and your undying love for each other. Tonight will mark your thirtieth year together. I wanted to involve the entire family here to create special memories for all of us, but I am already sure of the three of you being here with me tonight in some way. I wanted to write a one-page memoir of the most special moments in our life together, and then I thought a single page would just not be enough. Finally, I thought of talking to you as words flow through my heart and wish you a very happy marriage anniversary.

'While most people appreciate their parents for giving them life, I thank all three of you, for Aamir too was a parent to me. In fact, he was the best at that. You were the kind of couple whom so many loved for your generosity and kindness to all, including Aamir, because of which he stood so strong after you left us. I still remember that your acts of goodness were the life in this house, and changed our moods when we were upset at not being taken to the jungle at times. Both of you still have an impact on my life and I wish that I prove myself to be a good human being with time. I am living, doing well and travelling the world, because you were incredible parents. The two of you loved me the most in this world. It is your tenderness and care that helped me grow up to be who I am today. In the short time that we spent together, we had what most people can only dream about. This place is surely magical.

'I once heard someone say that they had never heard their parents fight. While I don't recall you ever throwing anything at each other and I suspect you did your best to hide your problems from us, I think a thirtieth wedding anniversary is a miracle deserving a very special tribute. Not only do most marriages not last that long, but few people last that long! I admire so much how you worked to stay together in good and bad times, till death. Not everybody is that lucky. That's how I think of it now.

'Mom and Dad, I've been thinking about your sacrifice, honesty, love, patience, gentleness, kindness, commitment and willingness to forgive. My memories of you are an inspiration to strive for the same in my marriage, if I am lucky enough to ever have one. You were blessed with the fortitude and faith to stay together, despite various forces that pull a couple apart. The example of your marriage reveals something much greater than any individual can ever attain. I hope all these memories will help me find my way.

'On this very special occasion of your thirtieth wedding anniversary, with a heart filled with the deepest gratitude, on behalf of Aamir and myself, please accept my honour, appreciation, admiration and love.

'I am here for a while, but I'm not sure when I'll come back and even though I wasn't here for long when I was a kid, I realize now that I missed our home more than I missed anything else in my life.

'May God continue to bless your marriage in heaven. May you enjoy your celebration tonight as I celebrate here. May you bless me through this year. I haven't seen Aamir for almost a month but I know my journey's not over yet, and you're always there, along with Aamir, blessing me for the best times in my life. I love you all,' he said, his eyes wet with tears, yet smiling.

When he finished talking, he moved back and reached for the water till he saw a cake that was a replica of the original anniversary cake. What he saw left him amazed. A video of the family that was put to music started with pictures of the parents as children and they were smiling. It continued with their wedding pictures and then came the childhood pictures of Aamir and Dhruv. This video kept playing for some minutes, reviving Dhruv's memories. He never wanted to let go of such beautiful memories. Then he saw poster boards containing family photos on easels all around the veranda.

He saw lanterns set alongside two wooden chairs; elegant and beautiful. He then saw silver helium balloons as centrepieces on the table, weighed down with Hershey's Kisses in silver foil covered in clear cellophane. There was music playing in the background. The table was covered with a white tablecloth with a large cake and a gift box kept on it. The original cake topper had also been used.

He then saw Sachi as she brought dishes, white paper plates and clear plastic flatware to the table on a tray. It was a simple celebration, yet she had created a very fun and friendly atmosphere.

'How did you manage to do all that? It is so special, Sachi,' Dhruv exclaimed.

It took a moment for her to answer. 'This is the least I could do, Dhruv. Trust me. And I just had to enter your house without your prior permission to do this. I collected all the details when you were out last evening.'

'It's unbelievable! You never told me that you were planning this all the while. What a lovely surprise, Sachi! There's no surprise more magical than this one! I couldn't be any happier. Thank you so much.'

'Okay. You can stop thanking me now and we can cut the cake for the best ever couple in the world.' She smiled, as they started off the celebration by cutting the cake.

'Did you do it yourself?'

She laughed. 'No, I have a secret team of people, living with me in that home, who helped me do it.'

He laughed back. 'I always thought I would do such things when I was a child, but it was too much. It would have taken some months to plan it all and do it. I am still amazed why you worked so hard.'

'I don't know. I just wanted to do this for you. This morning, when you were missing your family, I thought of reminding you about people who loved you and who still love you. Something came to mind, I went to Kanhal to buy a few necessary things and didn't take time to think before doing it.'

He smiled, took a sip of the juice and then told her about his relationship with Vratika, and how difficult it had been for him knowing her to be a reason for Aamir's accident.

'Dhruv, you now need to emerge from this hopelessness, and stop relating things to Aamir's death. It's done. And no power in the world will bring him back. You should rather cherish all the time you spent together, and think about being a different, mature and helpful person, who can actually make a difference in somebody's life. At the end of the day, your life is interesting and successful if you are remembered with love and gratitude after your death. Look for people who genuinely need help; you can be the one who fulfils that need. The satisfaction you get will be your guiding light till the end of your journey. There never seems to be enough time to help everybody, but we can at least try and make the most out of it. The least we can do is to hope to end up with the right regrets.'

'I'm sure I can do it now, Sachi, though I don't really know what to do. But I'll be a better person; I will try and be Aamir for some Dhruv in this world. There are plenty of people who need help and I am not going to let go this time.'

'Let me know if I can give you a hand with anything.'

'Certainly, though you've already done so much for me. No words can express my gratitude to you. I really haven't been myself lately. My mind has been drifting towards negativity. I would've lost it without you. Thank you for standing by me.'

'Dhruv, just because I've tried making this day special for both of us doesn't mean you have to praise me so much.'

'Yeah, but I need you to know how happy I am today,' he said as he watched her carefully.

'I'm just not sure whether you'll still be the same person when I am gone in a couple of days. But promise me that you'll always be happy.'

'I am going to miss you. I don't want to think of your leaving.' He said, and by his tone, she knew he was just making conversation; yet for some reason, the knowledge of her leaving made Dhruv feel lonely already.

Her face softened. 'I may leave, Dhruv, but you know I'll always come back.'

As he listened to her, he wondered again why she had come and done so much for him, especially when he needed someone around. Her conversation did not lead him to think she was in love with him. She came out of thin air, made his life easier and gave him a new hope to live his life. But none of that seemed to make much sense to him. It seemed to him that there was some great force that had directed him to her with the intention of bringing them together for a special purpose. Dhruv underwent a series of emotional changes during the second week of August. He began to spend most of his time with Sachi and enjoyed doing so. He loved her presence. He had begun to think that he was finally emerging from his shell and becoming himself again.

Dhruv realized that his time in Brahmi with Sachi would soon end. He couldn't imagine going back and resuming his life in

Mumbai. He longed for Sachi's presence in his life. Without her, he felt he was living estranged in a dark, cold abyss. He recalled how excited he had been when he first went to work in his office in Mumbai. Now, it meant nothing to him. His world revolved around Sachi, who had brought him back to life from his grief and depression. She was the most beautiful thing that ever happened to him. Her beauty was not merely physical; it was a combination of her thoughts, her lively and sparkling eyes, her interest in the things she loved, her ability to make others smile when she herself was sad, and her soul.

9 August 2006

He looked at the stars and thought about the plan to visit the temple with Sachi. He snapped out of his thoughts when he saw Sachi waving at him from a distance. He walked up to her and they exchanged a smile. He wanted to hug her and tell her how wonderful it was to be with her for all this time and how important she was, but thought better of it.

'Here, take this,' she said, giving him a beautiful handmade greeting card. 'I want you to have it.'

Dhruv was moved by the words scribbled on the card – 'Let this be an end to your sadness. It's time. Don't be so certain that you are 'unfixable'. Look around you – everyone is broken. If you continue to wear the label, then that's all you will ever be. You are allowed to be alive and happy. And never stop believing in miracles, because miracles happen every day. Wasn't our meeting here a miracle? Smile and move on, because you can.'

'You've rendered me speechless, Sachi. I wish I had something in return for you.'

'Your smile is all I need,' she answered.

'I owe you all the happiness I have and will ever have,' he said with a smile and tear-filled eyes.

'You are a great person, Dhruv. You deserve to be happy. Now, let's go to the temple,' saying that, she set off. Dhruv stared at her and then took large, quick steps to catch up with her. The temple was a few miles away, atop a hill. Dhruv finally told Sachi how much he wanted to stay close to her so that she could watch over him and ensure that he didn't fall back into depression.

He stared at the temple staircase, where he saw '20-05' engraved. Strangely, it was Aamir's birth date. It was hard to make an assumption based on this, so he just smiled and said, 'It feels so right to be here. Let's go.'

'Dhruv, I'll wait for you here. This is your call. You have to go by yourself,' her voice was firm.

'Are you sure? You could come,' Dhruv spoke, surprised at Sachi's decision.

'Yes, I am sure. Now you get going. It's already late.'

Dhruv didn't say anything; he went ahead alone. The temple stood intact after all those years. It was very beautiful with an aura of stillness and peace enshrouding every corner. Every moment spent there seemed to pacify his soul. Dhruv spent some time in the temple, remembering and praying for his family. When he walked out of the temple, he stole one more glance at the date '20-05' inscribed upon the stair. He wondered if it was just a coincidence.

As he moved forward, his eyes caught sight of a beautiful cherry blossom flower in the distance. It was Aamir's favourite flower. Dhruv was astonished to see it there; it grew in bunches in the month of November and yet there it was, a single flower sparkling in its full bloom in the month of July. He couldn't help but move in its direction. When Sachi saw him going the other way, she called out to him.

'Sachi, I've noticed unusual signs since we got here. First, that date inscribed on the stair, then a strong sensation inside the temple and now that flower growing out of season. These are all connected to Aamir in some way.'

'What do you mean?'

'I mean, there's far more to it than you or I could ever understand. I have to find that magic tree, which lets you connect to the spirits of your loved ones.

'It is already too late, Dhruv. We should be heading back now. Try to think rationally,' Sachi said in a loud voice, full of concern.

This is my chance to know if Aamir is still alive. I can't risk losing it.' Dhruv turned away and walked ahead.

'What do you possibly mean by *that?* You only told me Aamir died in a terrorist attack last month.'

'Yes, I did. But that's what the police told me. I searched for him everywhere and couldn't find him, Sachi. I had never been able to see him one last time or do his last rituals. I accepted his death with time but I feel something around here. And if he's dead, he'll speak to me, Sachi.'

'You never really discussed this with me, Dhruv. In the first place, were you mad accepting your brother's death just like that? Without any evidence?' Sachi said.

'Sachi, can we please discuss this later? You have to admit the world works in mysterious ways. There are things beyond our logic and rational explanations. I have this feeling, and I can't give up on it.' Dhruv knew he was doing the right thing. He couldn't ignore his intuition. He knew the mind could play tricks, that love was blind, but gut feelings were mostly right. He was shaking up with determination. Sachi had to finally give in and follow his lead.

He was eager to discover what lay behind the story of the magical tree. He noted everything that came his way. He wondered what it would be like to find that tree in reality; he wondered whether it existed or was just another local legend. He did believe what he'd been told by Mr. Das, and kept searching. He continued to look from one tree to another. It was getting late, but the atmosphere was elegantly beautiful.

'I think we're moving in the wrong direction; we should go in the opposite direction from here,' Sachi said in a quiet, low voice.

'How can you be so sure, Sachi? I think we're going the right way. I can't see anything in the opposite direction.'

'It's because I study these things, and such things are mostly located where they are expected the least, so that spirits can connect with you without any hurdles from the existing world. I think there's no harm in giving it a try,' she replied.

They turned around and headed in the opposite direction. As they moved further away from the road and the temple, the forest grew denser. They could easily hear the sound of crickets, and other animals moving around with leaves crumbling under their feet. They both knew if they ventured too far, it could prove to be very dangerous. They were risking their lives. They could feel every single moment ticking away with every step they took.

He suddenly felt a feather brushing his face gently. It didn't fall down; instead, it continued to fly in the direction in which they were walking, as if to tell him that they were on the right path. Sachi walked at his side, completely engaged in trying to locate the tree. Suddenly, she tripped over a stone and lost her balance. She called out to Dhruv. He tried to grip her waist to balance her, but instead, they both lost their balance and rolled down the hill for a few seconds, till Dhruv grabbed a tree and gripped Sachi as well. 'Are you okay?' Dhruv was out of breath and had gone pale due to his concern for her.

'Ah, yes, I guess I am. It's alright. Just some bruises,' Sachi replied in a breathless voice. She took Dhruv's hand to get back on her feet. She looked dishevelled.

As they got up and moved ahead, they saw something which amazed them. It was as if they had escaped into a wonderland. It was difficult to believe their eyes. The sight was soothing them in ways they could never define in words… like a beautiful song whose lyrics they had forgotten but the music continued to echo in their minds. They had never seen anything quite so beautiful earlier. The more they looked at it, the more they wanted to get into it. They had only heard about such places in age-old stories narrated by their grandparents or seen them in a children's fantasy books. The very fact of it being real made them stare at it for longer.

It was a tree on the edge of a beautiful pond. It sparkled in the dark night, more brightly than the moon. As they drew closer to it, they felt as if they were being protected with something very sacred, as if the area around the tree was being saved from all the evil spirits of the world and making it a hallowed place for divine spirits. They could feel the breeze that moved through the branches of the tree as it touched their bodies. A purifying aura engulfed their bodies, minds and souls. The stars were at their brightest and colourful fishes jumped happily out of the pond as if they were blessed to live forever. The grass tickled their bare feet as they walked over fallen leaves. Dewdrops fell on their heads from the leaves on the trees.

'Have you ever seen anything more beautiful than this?' Dhruv asked as he faced her.

'Not even at my most imaginative,' she replied all dreamy-eyed.

They fell silent as they moved closer to the tree. So much had happened in the past few minutes. It was probably the moment for which Dhruv had been waiting all along but still couldn't believe what he saw. He gripped the tree, and wept unashamedly. Sachi smiled at him from a distance. She knew Dhruv had several wishes to talk about.

He had been humming something to the tree, as if asking for a wish to come true, or work as a messenger. He kept on humming as Sachi watched him from a distance. Suddenly the magical tree emitted brighter light and a stronger fragrance, which made Dhruv nostalgic. As he concentrated on it, he realized that it was the same fragrance that Aamir used to wear. He was shaken at the very thought of it. Teary-eyed, he called out in a whisper, 'Aamir, are you here?'

Dhruv's fists were clenched tightly and he hoped the old man had spoken the truth. He didn't want the story of the magical tree to be an illusion. He was sobbing and calling out for Aamir. He got down on his knees, closed his eyes and called out again in a shaking voice, 'Brother, please talk to me. I can't take it anymore. I need you. I am very sorry. Forgive me.' He couldn't stop trembling and crying, not until he heard a voice.

'Stop blaming yourself, Dhruv. It wasn't your fault. It was just an unfortunate accident.' Dhruv froze. He couldn't bring himself to believe that he was actually hearing what he had longed to hear. But it wasn't the voice he was expecting, and the voice he was certain he would never hear again. Was all that really happening? It was the voice of his father.

'Dad, is that you? How's Aamir? How's mom? Please come back. Don't leave me alone. I promise to follow every single thing you say. I will never again cause trouble or be irresponsible or misbehave. Just come back.'

'Yes, Dhruv. It's me. You have to pull yourself together and move on to understand certain things that you're missing out on. You have to give up self criticism and defeating self-talk, then only you'll find it all. You are so much braver and smarter than you give yourself credit for. There's much more to know, much more to discover.'

'I never realized what I had until Aamir was gone. I don't do the same things now. I don't even know what I am doing most time ever since he's gone. I don't know how I ended up coming to Brahmi. My life is in a complete mess.'

'No, Dhruv. You're doing everything over here for a reason. You came here to get to your roots, to fulfil somebody's wish and experience your childhood. That's appreciable. You've come farther and things must have changed for you, but you're doing good, Dhruv. This world has rules that you must follow and you'll get all your answers with time.'

Dhruv listened to him in pained silence for some time. All he could see was the look in Sachi's eyes and all he could hear was his father's voice

He heard his father speaking again, 'Listen, Dhruv, the past can't be erased, edited, rejected or forgotten. It can only be accepted. I want you to make peace with whatever has happened. I want you to take care of yourself and live your life, happily, completely, without fear and regrets. You've much more to know which I can't tell you; you need to find it out by yourself. You need to believe that your destiny is tied up with other people's destiny. If you have a genuine purpose to live for, you'll get it all.'

He felt as if his father was giving him some indications and had put his hand on his shoulder.

'I can't do this. I can't do this without all of you. Please tell me how's Aamir?' he whispered softly as tears ran down his cheeks.

'Of course you can and you already are. Be strong, for your family, for Aamir, for your future and for your difficult past. Always remember, you've not lost everything still. You just have to realize it and be alert. You need to keep your search going for Aamir. Try to figure out the right course of action as you move through these incredibly challenging times. This is your chance. The chance to forgive, to do better, to do more, to give more, to love more. To stop worrying about 'what if' and start embracing 'what will be'. Promise us, you'll never give up on your life. Can you do that for us?'

Dhruv couldn't believe what he had just heard. He nodded his head several times and said, wiping away his tears, 'Yes! Yes, I will. I promise you. I'll keep searching for him.'

'It is so good that you decided to come here to Brahmi.'

'I owe even this to Aamir. Had Aamir not discussed it with me that day, I would have never been here. Thank you, dad, for everything. I am so lucky that I still have you watching over me.' Dhruv felt blessed, for very few get a chance to let their loved ones know they are missed after they are gone. 'Dad, can I do something for you?'

'Yes, there are certainly some unfulfilled wishes of mine. You'll get to know about them in time and I am sure you'll try your best to fulfil those.'

'I'll do anything. I will do even the impossible for you.'

'For now, I need you to resume your life back in Mumbai. Come here when you can, but other than that, you need to start your life all over again and follow your instincts. That will lead you somewhere out of your imagination. I want to see you happy with someone with whom you can share your life. I want you to start a family. And don't forget to remind yourself that you deserve a lot of happiness; that I will always love you and watch over you.'

'Is this a goodbye?'

'There will never be a goodbye, Dhruv. We're always tied together. It's a promise which will never be withdrawn.'

Dhruv smiled and a cold breeze touched his face and wrapped itself around him. It was a celebration. It was a night of wonders which few have experienced in their lifetime and still doubt if it exists.

He saw Sachi standing some distance away. He didn't speak, but hugged her instead. Sachi smiled at him and said, 'I think your father said it all. Whatever happened was magic and I think there couldn't be a better ending to this trip. I guess it's time for both of us to move ahead and re-think certain things.'

He felt thirsty; he felt his sweaty hand suddenly slipping down his bed. He recollected one sequence after another and immediately opened his eyes to find that it was nothing else but a dream. He turned on the lights; he needed to relax. But he knew that sleep wouldn't come. His dream was not just the images he saw. He believed it had much to do with reality. The magical tree, the temple, and his father signalling towards Aamir couldn't simply be put as mere co-incidence or a dream.

He shook his head, numb. He knew he'd have to find answers to all these questions. His hands were shaking. He needed somebody to talk to, and more importantly, he needed somebody to just second his thoughts. He looked around for Sachi. He called out to her when he saw the door of her home open. He noticed that the lights were on, but there was nobody there.

He left home because he didn't find Sachi there.

He checked his watch; it was 2.00 a.m. He wondered where Sachi would have gone off to, so late at night. There was nobody out at this hour apart from him. After taking a walk for some time, he knocked another door without any second thought. There was no response for some time. He decided to walk back before he heard a voice, 'Dhruv! You're here at this hour? Is everything ok?' Mr. Das asked, clearly surprised.

'Hi,' he replied. 'I wanted to meet you' He said quietly, not knowing what else to say.

'Are you okay?'

'I don't know,' he almost whispered.

'You look like you've been hit by sudden trauma. Please tell me what happened.'

Dhruv stayed silent for some time and stood in front of him.

'I'm glad that you came, Dhruv.' Mr. Das patted his shoulder and ushered him in. 'But please tell me what happened to you.'

'Maybe I shouldn't have come; it was just a dream anyway. I should go, I shouldn't be disturbing you,' he said, shaking his head.

'What dream? And I am sure if you've come to meet me at this hour, it's something serious and meaningful. Please tell me.'

As they took their seats in the spacious living room, Dhruv told him everything about the dream, the images he'd seen of the magical tree, his conversation with Sachi and his father. Mr. Das sat quietly as he talked, his experienced eyes observing his emotions, fear and hope. Dhruv did his best to explain everything that he remembered and looked relaxed as he vented it all out.

Mr. Das nodded. 'I don't want to make any false promises here. But I certainly see some message in store for you'

'But what can be the possible message behind all this?'

'As you mentioned, Aamir was declared dead by the police and you didn't witness it by yourself. I see lots of hope here, Dhruv.'

'I tried almost everything to find him, but there wasn't any clue of him. Plus, why would the police lie?'

'No! That's not what I mean to say. They aren't lying. But they considered Aamir one of those dead bodies which were left unidentified. Aamir might not be one of those.'

'I hope so too. But that doesn't really narrow down the possibility of him being alive as well.'

'It's true, though. It's anyway a hope if we feel that it wasn't just a dream. I remember my dad telling me stories about the pure connection between dream and reality.'

'You believed them then?'

'I used to believe every word of it then, but as I grew up, I made myself believe that there's no such thing and I guess, I was wrong to not believe them lately.'

'I don't know what to say or do now.'

'You'd certainly not like to live with a feeling of never having tried to search Aamir for one last time. As your dream said, take life as it comes and follow your instinct.' Mr. Das said sincerely, asking Dhruv to keep his search on for Aamir. They discussed it for quite a while.

Most men wouldn't have done what Mr. Das had done for him till now. He was content to know about the old man's view too. Without a word more, he hugged him and asked for his blessings.

For a moment, he lost track of what was happening. But he decided to take a step ahead before beginning to follow his instincts. He decided to go back Mumbai as soon as he could. He walked back home in silence. Dhruv shed a few tears on the way back, but this time, he cried for joy. Not because he felt guilty or defeated, but because now he hoped that Aamir was still alive somewhere.

Eventually, as his eyes blurred, he went off to sleep, turning his face to the moon.

He thought in his mind as he often pondered about the mystery in his life, he was a finite who had to understand the infinite. A ray of hope was still shining in that darkest hour.

9 August 2006

In the darkness of the night, Sachi kept her eyes on the road as she walked on. She'd enjoyed spending time in Brahmi, which she found to be a magical place. She had learnt long ago that no one gets everything that they want in life. Therefore, it was always best to stop regretting the small stuff and get on in life. She thought of the things Rahil and she would've done in Brahmi, on their own. But she reminded herself that the life of which she was dreaming was gone and she could do nothing about it. Taking a deep breath, she took out a picture and looked at it for some time. She ran her fingers over it. She didn't have a night like that before.

It was a dark windy night; she wasn't willing to go back yet. It was as if she wanted to be blown by that one wind to

Rahil forever. Struggling with these thoughts, she sat for some time at the lake, and tossed pebbles into the water. The sound of the water made her realize that everything runs its course. Nature provides an example of how life goes on. Everything and everyone that one encountered in life had a purpose; when the purpose is fulfilled, something else or someone else comes along, to fulfil a new purpose and continue the journey. She closed her eyes as she thought about Rahil; how he came into her life like a warm breeze that blew away all her bad memories and replaced them with delightful recollections. She always liked having him around and appreciated the way he cared for her. He always knew how to make her smile.

She remembered how, when they had first met, Rahil had talked on one topic or another to her, to impress her. It almost took him forever to propose to her as he was shy with women. Sometimes she wondered what she would have been like if Rahil had never come into her life. It wouldn't have been easy for her. She knew she'd always been right about Rahil. He was the only person in her life, she thought, who understood her completely. She recalled several wonderful moments that she had shared with Rahil. She was beginning to feel dizzy and her mouth had gone dry when she recalled that one incident that separated them forever.

She couldn't remember much about that night. She couldn't even remember how he had died so suddenly, before her very eyes. She didn't even get time to take him to the hospital. A fatal disease and that was all. Now that she had trouble living between reality and dreams, she wanted to go back to Rahil and say the words she had wished to speak. She wanted reality to be presented to the world. Against all odds, she knew it could happen; somebody she knew could still do it for her.

I think he loves me, she thought. As quickly as those thoughts came, she dismissed them, thinking it ridiculous. But then, she thought, it wasn't really that hard to believe. It could happen, for he had been through a difficult time for some months and she was probably expecting this. When Dhruv looked at her, she could sense love, care and unsaid words in his eyes. She always watched him carefully. It was as if she could almost read his mind before he said a word. She knew when he expected her to hold his hand, when he expected her to stop him from doing something. She was always there as if it was meant to be. A great force had directed her towards Dhruv, even though she didn't want to believe it. Deep down, she could sense that Dhruv had developed strong feelings for her.

Quietly, she began her walk back home. It was very late at night and she hadn't been back since morning. She knew that although it was so late at night, Dhruv might expect her to spend some time with him. Sachi wondered again if Dhruv would be able to live his life normally after he returned to Mumbai. Although she wanted things to return to normal, she knew it wasn't easy for her or for Dhruv. She knew that they'd both leave Brahmi in a few days; this would be the hardest goodbye of her life. She was missing him already, and she knew that despite the differences in their lives, she would always go back to Dhruv whenever he needed her.

As she returned home, she saw Dhruv sleeping outside. She gazed at him, smiling regretfully. She didn't know what to say. She remained quiet and wondered what he must be thinking of in his dreams.

10 August 2006

Dhruv washed his face and hands and shaved quickly as he thought of meeting Sachi. Ten minutes later, he walked to her home. It was ten in the morning. He knocked on the door, and she opened the door after what seemed like a never-ending wait. She had tied her hair into a neat ponytail and wore no makeup. Her simplicity made her look even more beautiful. Dhruv just stood there, gazing at her, awe-struck. There was something wonderfully pure and innocent about his interest in Sachi. He shook his head to come out of his trance and asked her, 'Where were you last night? I dozed off waiting for you. There were so many things to talk about!'

'Oh, I am so sorry. I should've waited for you or informed you at least. I was missing Rahil a lot and wanted to spend some time alone.' She spoke very delicately. Her creamy skin glowed golden in the sun rays falling in from the door, her long hair moved swiftly in the morning breeze, occasionally touching her face. She looked straight into Dhruv's eyes.

'We live quite close to each other, Sachi. You could have told me. I'm not sure whether I am right but there has to be a reason for our being here. I was so worried last night.' Dhruv's tone expressed his concern and anger.

Sachi took the hint and apologized, 'I am very sorry...I did not intend to cause you worry. I wanted to tell you, but I only returned in the morning.'

'Ah, I hope I haven't overdone it. It's okay. I am just relieved that you are safe.' He wanted to say many more things but couldn't. He knew she was special for him, a feeling that couldn't be defined or confined in words. She fitted his concept of a perfect lady. She had come into his life as the break of a dawn arrives after a dark night. He knew he couldn't keep her with him forever; each day they spent together brought the day of their parting closer. He couldn't bring himself to accept that in a few days' time, she would no longer be a part of his life. Last night, he had glimpsed the turmoil her absence would bring into his life. She was his joy, his laughter, his companion. He had begun to believe that he couldn't spend a day without a glimpse of her smile, talking to her and listening to the sound of her voice. He knew the clock was ticking; he was running out of time and so he wanted to be with her as much as possible.

'I guess you want to say something, Dhruv.' She smiled and said this when she saw him staring into the distance, lost in his thoughts.

'Yes, it is about someone I met yesterday after a dream that I saw,' Dhruv said to change the subject. They began to stroll in the front yard as Dhruv described his dream and his meeting with Mr. Das. He spoke of the temple and the magic tree. Dhruv was filled with anticipation at the thought of what the last day in Brahmi and life ahead had in store for him.

Sachi seldom spoke or moved until Dhruv said something, but today she noticed the needy expression on his face as she sincerely listened to him for an hour. She was surprised to hear it all. She said, 'I'm positive you'll find him.'

Dhruv nodded. 'I wish I had some connection with him. I'm not even sure whether it's true, but I would certainly like to give it a try. I wish I had done it earlier.'

'You've been spending a lot of time thinking about them lately. I am sure this wasn't just a dream. Once you find him, he'll be glad to know that you put the heavens and earth together to find him.'

'I too hope the same. But what makes you so certain? Are you saying this based on your intuition or on a personal experience?'

'I say this because I think it's possible and I'd like you to believe that it's true too. There's a world beyond set logics and principles which never fails to amaze you.'

'That's pretty philosophical. But yes, I think so too. May be I'll take the train to Mumbai tomorrow itself.'

'Great, I too have my train tomorrow itself. Do you want me to help with something?'

'I don't want to say no to you, but you've already done a lot for me, I think I'll manage on my own.'

'Are you sure?'

'Yes, you're a great friend and you mean a lot to me. In fact, I wanted to tell you…'

Sachi shifted her feet slightly and interrupted him. 'I think I will finish my walk and we'll catch up in the evening.'

'Sure…some food, a long talk and then a silent walk. See you then.' She cut his point off and walked away.

Maybe he wanted to say something to Sachi, but he knew there was nothing he could do to help himself there. He did not want to leave her. He wondered if he had developed some feelings for Sachi or maybe he was afraid of losing her. He stared at her as she walked back to her home and thought of going inside to speak to her. But something stopped him from doing so. He'd often wondered what it would be like to have Sachi with him.

A little while later, he thought of how his life would change on his return to Mumbai. Consciously or unconsciously, he'd been leading a life in the last few days that would lead him to be a better and more mature person.

❀

11 August 2006

Time had seemed to move swiftly in the last some nights for Dhruv. If he were to describe the events of that night to someone, he might not have believed. But that really didn't matter to Dhruv anymore. That dream and the brief interaction with Mr. Das had changed his life forever and paved a new path for him. Dhruv was quiet and calm that morning while packing his bags. He occasionally touched the furniture his father had bought some decades ago, as he knew he wouldn't be there after a while.

He sat on his father's wooden chair. He wasn't certain about what he would do, but he knew he had to honour his father's last words. He took out Aamir's picture and kissed it with a smile. A few days back, when he had come to Brahmi, he was broken, disturbed, and clueless about what he was doing, where he was going, who he was. Now, he had answers to all those questions. He had a new meaning for his life. He felt like living for an eternity in those few days. His father made it clear in his dream that he was missing out on something he had given up on. He now had a new ray of hope; his father had given him hope by not making anything clear about Aamir.

He came out into the veranda and found Sachi standing in hers. She was simply looking around, sipping tea from a cup. Her hair was untied, very tangled and messy, giving her such a dreamy-hazy look. The only thing Dhruv could think of was why he hadn't met her years ago. Sachi spotted Dhruv staring at her. She smiled and walked towards him.

Dhruv looked more relaxed and happy than any other day. Seeing that, Sachi asked in her softest tone possible, 'How are you feeling?'

'I guess I can't explain. But I am certainly feeling different. I know it's going to be strange for me whenever I think about that dream, but I guess that's what this probably is about. A new hope there, it looks like a re-birth of mine. I want to rush to Mumbai soon now.'

'I know, I've never seen you so well before as I have in the last two days. It's like a medication that worked. But yes, I really hope that this is not a passing phase. Whenever I think about last to last night, I see this happy face of yours and not the one I saw when I first met you. I hope whatever your dream said brings out happiness for you and it just keeps you happy and healthy, Dhruv.'

'I really hope for the same.' Dhruv was genuinely smiling.

They sat in silence for a while. It was a somewhat uncomfortable silence. They exchanged unspoken words every time their eyes met, every moment they breathed, and each movement they made. They both knew that they had ventured too far. Sensing the direction in which the conversation could go, Sachi abruptly got up to go back. 'I will see you in a while. I am yet to pack my stuff and take care of a couple more things.'

'It's fine. I am almost done. You call me whenever you're done, we'll leave then,' he replied. She nodded in response and left quickly.

11 August 2006

It was a cosy and cold evening. Dhruv left Mr. Das's house at sundown, bidding the older man farewell, returning his keys and walking back home to pick Sachi, who was ready to leave too. Before leaving, he met the restaurant owner, who had kept his food ready for the journey. Dhruv promised to come back soon. They both talked for a while before Sachi called, 'Dhruv, we're getting late.'

He got back quickly and as he moved, he watched the branches of trees dancing in the wind, preparing them for the rain tonight. As he walked, he replayed the events of his days, thinking not only that but also about Mr. Das, who had been so kind to him. Like him, Mr. Das had no family left in the world, which was why he wanted Dhruv to return to Brahmi. It was the first time he had ever spoken to someone other than Aamir about his father. His thoughts then shifted to Sachi. He felt that by spending time with her in the last few days, he'd got his real self back. She had helped him recover much that had been good about his childhood, many memories that he had lost after the death of his parents. He hoped she would not leave and that they would meet again after a few days. He had never been the type of person to think of such things earlier.

Dhruv took one last look at his home and then they started their journey to Kanhal. They decided to walk part of the way. As they did, Dhruv smelled the same fragrance he had smelt near the tree. He knew it was his father who had just passed by him to give his blessings. He smiled and kept walking.

They didn't talk at all until they had covered almost half the distance. Dhruv finally broke the silence, 'Sachi, we'll soon part and go our ways. There's very little time left.'

'I'm not leaving you here, Dhruv.' She spoke in her angelic voice. 'We'll be in touch. I'll keep an eye on you and if our schedules permit, we'll meet. You aren't going to be alone. I am always there for you. Trust me, it's not going to be any different.'

'It will be very different, Sachi. We won't go for walks, exchange stories or have celebrations together. We won't even know what we will be doing for most of the time. I will be surprised if we meet again. You won't be there to cheer me up if I again get lost in one of those stressful and disheartening days in Mumbai.'

'Dhruv, everybody gets used to it. Initially, we'll certainly miss each other. But if we don't meet very often, we'll adjust to the regular schedule. That's one established pattern of life.'

'That's a mean thing to say,' Dhruv said, looking hurt. 'How could you think that it would be so easy after getting to know me?'

'No, Dhruv. I didn't mean to hurt you. I wish I was living and working in Mumbai and we could meet every day. But we live in different places, which are very distant from each other. No matter how hard we try, we can't really overcome that.' Sachi looked at him in pained silence for a long time.

'This is no time to hide behind words, Sachi. I know you have your own life and I have mine, and we have no common ground on which we can connect, but if we both give it a try, I am sure things can be worked out even if we are a million miles apart.'

'Yes, I agree. We could still make it work, if we wanted to.'

'I hope it stays that way. I've already lost too many loved ones in my life now. I can't afford to lose anybody else. Sachi, if we try our best, we'll eventually make it happen and if we lose it now, we'll lose it forever. I don't want that to happen. I don't want to give up. Since we've spent so much time together in the last few days, I am certain that if things remain stable, we can make it work out for both of us. You know what I mean to say?'

She didn't say a word, so he continued, 'Sachi, before we part, I want you to know something.'

'I guess I already know it, Dhruv. We're good friends. You know that.'

'Yes, Sachi. But you mean a lot to me now and you know that.' He said everything that had been unspoken between them. He had finally mustered the courage to tell her that he wanted more from the relationship. In some ways, it was a relief for him to say this.

'Dhruv, I don't think there's any chance of that happening. And you know the reason why.' She spoke as if she was fighting for the right words.

'Sachi, I understand it's difficult for you. But if we give it up now, you'll probably end the likelihood of getting along with anybody in your life. In fact, it isn't easy for me either, but…'

He was cut short by Sachi, 'We can talk about all this later someday.'

'Then why are you running away from it? What's wrong in talking about it, Sachi? There's so much that I wanted to talk about.'

'I am not running away from it, Dhruv. You're my dearest friend and I just think that it's not the right time to talk about it.'

'I respect your opinion. Yet I'm not willing to pretend that we'll go our own ways in a few hours, get back to our own lives and that would be that. I don't want to hide my feelings. I just want to express the care and affection I've developed for you, Sachi and I want you to know that.'

'You need to give it a lot of thought before you say anything like this, Dhruv. You know about Rahil and me. Don't you?'

'Of course, I do. And I respect your relationship as well, but you need to move on now. Unfortunately, he's no more and you can't spend all your life just thinking about him.'

A part of Sachi had died with Rahil. She spent her life reliving her moments with Rahil, unable to believe that it was over between them. It felt right to her to be alone, to owe her happiness and grief to Rahil and no one else. She was no longer at that point in her life where she could love someone else. She could not say all this to Dhruv, for it went against everything that she had tried to convey to him in their time together. Dhruv, on the other hand, was intense and emotional; he believed her to be a very strong woman, with a great understanding of life. Although he knew she had been passionately in love with Rahil, he also knew he had a chance with her since Rahil wasn't there anymore. He didn't want to give up on the possibility of being with her.

After a prolonged silence, Dhruv spoke again, 'Hey, please don't think I am trying to force anything on you. We share the most beautiful friendship in its truest form. We are at that point in our lives where we need to relate to somebody who is genuine and loyal to care for us. We need that kind of support, don't we?'

'Yes, that is true. But that's not the only thing that you expect from a relationship. Do you?'

Dhruv looked down to avoid responding.

Sachi tried to explain to him that she needed more time. She was not yet out of love with Rahil. She was not certain if she could feel the same way for someone else. Moreover, she didn't want to be unfair to Dhruv, hurt his feelings and jeopardize their friendship. She was certain she cared about him, but it was a tough call. 'Dhruv, I would be no less hurt if we never get to see each other again. But now you need to concentrate on many other things. Remember that dream of yours? Time has come when you need to focus all your energies somewhere else.'

'Finding somebody whom I love and who loves me is one of the promises.'

'You just said "somebody who loves me", so that's still half done at this moment.'

'And I want that too. You're the one who holds my life,' he said bluntly and innocently, and she couldn't suppress her smile.

'Look, there's nobody who holds anybody's life here. Everyone's got their lives in their own hands. Don't ignore reality and enjoy the time we have together.'

'Maybe I ask for too much from you.'

'I never said that,' she said, paused and resumed speaking again. 'Well, maybe, we can promise to meet here once every year for a few days, just like we did this time.'

'You know that's not what I want. That's just not enough,' he said stubbornly.

'All right, can you do one thing?'

'Anything.'

She smiled and said, 'I just want you to reconsider your decision when you return to Mumbai. And, if you still want us to be together and are certain about it, I'll come to Mumbai to discuss it further. But for now, you know what needs to be done.'

Dhruv's joy knew no bounds when he heard her say this. He was certain that what he felt for Sachi was real and it couldn't disappear after he resumed his life in Mumbai. Sachi's assurance made his heart dance in delight. They continued their journey, talking and reliving the moments they had shared together. The days seemed to have passed so quickly. Dhruv even talked about his life in Mumbai and his earlier relationships, this time casually and without any tears or regret in his eyes. After they reached the highway, they boarded a bus to Kanhal.

On reaching Kanhal, they both bought their tickets at the station. Dhruv's train was to arrive before Sachi's. They sat on the platform in an emotional and painful silence. All Dhruv could think of was how lucky he was to have met her and come to Brahmi. He had never really thought talking to his dad ever again would be a possibility, but Brahmi had made it possible.

'I am going to get some tea. You need anything?' Dhruv asked.

'A cup of tea for me too; it's so cold already.'

Dhruv came back with two steaming cups of tea. 'Here we go...special tea for both of us.'

As soon as he handed her the glass, it fell. 'Oh, I am so sorry. I just couldn't hold it. My hands are numb with the cold,' she said.

'That's fine. I'll get another one for you,' he said, and turned to get another glass.

'No need; we'll share it. I don't want much.'

'Are you sure?'

'Yes, totally.' She said, smiled and winked at him.

They sipped the tea in silence, watching each other. They'd matured a lot over the past month. Silence no longer bothered them. They didn't find it awkward. They didn't need constant conversation to comfort and distract them. But there was a possibility of an emotional breakdown if they continued to gaze at each other so intensely. Sachi finally looked away. Both of them were relieved.

Dhruv truly admired Sachi. People like her were so rare to find. She was selfless and did not believe in faking or disguising her feelings. She was an incredibly understanding and patient woman who also understood the reason behind everything that had happened last night and didn't ask Dhruv anything. Dhruv conveyed all these feelings to her. 'People don't care for their relatives and you helped a complete stranger!'

'I disagree. I think everybody in the world helps you in some way or the other, intentionally or unintentionally. But you never know what the other person really expects from you. They might or might not say it outright; it's their choice. But it's as true as oxygen in the air.'

'Then tell me…what do you expect from me?'

'If you really want to know, then I expect you to work really hard, and with all your heart. Live, learn, laugh and love as much as you can.'

'Your wish is my command, ma'am. I will take care of it.' They both shared a laugh. Dhruv started counting backwards for the minutes left for his train to arrive.

'Thanks,' she said.

'Will you remember this time after a few years? Will it matter?'

'It certainly will, even after decades,' she said, putting strands of hair behind her ears.

He was still certain that his going back to Mumbai would bring about a positive change in his life. The events of the previous night and this evening were still too fresh in his mind. The memories that they made there would be long lasting. He took out the picture from his wallet yet again and kissed for sheer joy. He was happy because the many questions to which no one had any answers apart from sympathy had been answered by his father himself.

He glanced around the station. He saw people – happy, sad, depressed and well-dressed. Some were waiting to receive somebody; some were there to see off their relatives. People held back their tears. Some were evidently looking at the rail tracks to check if there were any trains coming. As it grew dark and the moon rose, people put on their sweaters to protect themselves from the cold.

For a moment he wondered what it would be like to settle in Brahmi and explore the opportunities of a life. What did one need to live? Peace, a home and a family to share it with. That would not be a bad idea to consider for the future.

And suddenly his thoughts were interrupted by the loud sound of a train's siren and the announcement of the train's arrival. He saw Sachi, who wasn't looking his way at all. But the change in her expression showed that she too had heard the horn. She slid Dhruv's bag forward, without looking at him, as if unwillingly asking him to leave. Dhruv got up, put his hands on her shoulder, smiled and said, 'Would you want to join me?' She didn't look up and shook her head in disagreement.

'This train will leave in two minutes. That's definitely not enough to say goodbye to you or to this place for the beautiful time I spent here with you. But I just want to say one thing – do remember me in your good days and hard times. I'll always be there with you. I'll call you when I reach Mumbai. Take care and yes, I care for you. Do pray for me and my brother.'

He stood up and looked at her intently, waiting for her to respond. But her expression was neutral. He placed his hand on her shoulder and kissed her forehead. Dhruv saw something which he had never seen in all the time he had spent with her. There were tears in her eyes, rolling down her cheeks, despite the blank expression on her face.

The others on the platform were staring at them.

He thought of embracing her, but the train's siren went off again and it started moving. With a heavy heart, he ran to catch the train and got on, turning back again and again to catch a last glimpse of her. He waved his hand several times, but she didn't respond and he soon lost sight of her.

He took his seat, got his ticket checked and started thinking about Sachi's sad face and teary eyes. He had never seen her like that earlier. She seemed to be so strong and focused, so unlike him. He couldn't get her hauntingly expressionless, yet sad face out of his mind. He identified her with her smile, her liveliness and her ability to motivate him; then how could she be so sad? He found it strange and painful.

However, he was fascinated by the way she had changed his life without imposing any kind of authority over it. Her ideas were so convincing. He lay down on his berth and recalled their relationship from the beginning – how they had met, their walks together, her positive attitude, the celebration of his parents' anniversary and that dream, which had made this journey so wonderful. As he thought of these things, he hoped to be together with Sachi.

12 August 2006

It was a morning unlike the past several mornings that Dhruv had spent in Brahmi. A lot had changed overnight for him. There were no birds chirping, there was little or no peace, and he did not awaken in heaven and go for a walk to the lake nearby. He was somewhat frightened by the crowd; he wanted to run back to Brahmi and never return. But Mumbai was his world now. He had spent most of his life there and would have to live there in the future.

As he switched on his mobile phone, he realized the train had reached its destination – Mumbai. He picked up his bag and got off the train. He had resigned himself to his life in the city which never says 'No'. Returning to Mumbai after a long break had been an overwhelming experience for him, but he didn't want to get lost amongst the millions of people there.

12 August 2006

As he reached home, he found it silent, as if all life had ended after he was gone. He lay down on his sofa, and took off his shoes. As he glanced around, he noticed Aamir's T-shirt, which he had been wearing the morning of his accident, still hanging there. It was his favourite, a blue round necked T-shirt. That was one t-shirt that he refused to share with Dhruv because it was gifted to him by Anvi.

He stood up, touched and sniffed at the t-shirt. It still smelled of Aamir and the fragrance he liked to use. He was determined to treasure it forever and never wash it. He gradually walked around the house and began putting things to rights; it reminded him of his house in Brahmi. Aamir's clothes were lying around; he carefully folded and put them in his cupboard. He occasionally touched and felt all of Aamir's clothes. He had been so brave when he made his promise to his father. He did not want to break down and weep now as he had hopes of finding him back. He got up, washed his face and sat on the balcony, where he and Aamir spent so much time together. That balcony had seen them laugh and weep often. He noticed that even though Aamir seldom spoke much, his home was strangely silent.

After some time, as he sipped some tea that he had prepared for himself, he realized he was so used to drinking tea that Aamir had prepared. He had gotten used to everything that was related to Aamir, but now he was on his own.

He took out his laptop to check e-mails and messages that had arrived in his absence.

The first one that caught his eye was from his office.

Dear Dhruv,

We understand that you were on leave till 16th August, after the regrettable demise of your brother. However, we need you to revert to us on this official mail. We've tried calling your number, but you're unreachable. You are requested to call back or inform us regarding the date of joining.

Ignoring this mail may lead to your termination from the job based on company policies and procedures.

Regards,

Rubeena
National Head

Dhruv realised that his phone might not have worked at all in Brahmi. He quickly put in a one-line reply to the email.

Dear Rubeena,

Thanks for writing in and your patience. I was travelling and was stationed at a remote destination, perhaps why you couldn't reach me.

I'll join office from 19th August.

Regards,

Dhruv

The next email was from Vratika.
He hesitated for just a moment before clicking it open.

Dhruv,

I tried calling and messaging you many times, but I couldn't reach you. I even visited your flat several times to see you, but I couldn't find you there either. I hope you're alright wherever you are. I am so worried about you.

I also want to tell you something, about Aamir's unfortunate accident. I know whatever I say will have little meaning for you and I might end up sounding ridiculous. But I am really sorry for whatever happened that day. Had it not been for me and my stupid behaviour that day, Aamir would still be alive. I know you must see me as that bitch who was responsible for all this, and you're not wrong. But trust me, I did not want this to happen. His death was as shocking for me as it was for you. I know I've hurt you much and no apology can bring Aamir back. I don't want to live with the guilt that I was responsible for the death of my boyfriend's brother – somebody who cared a lot for me and gave me everything in life that I never really deserved. I miss you. I never knew you'd go so far away from my life.

It seems so unfair to say this to you at this moment, but would you please give me one more chance in life, Dhruv? Please write back to me. I need to know that you're fine and doing well. I love you. I am sorry if I don't sound sensible. Please forgive me if you can.

I hope you write back.

Vratika

Dhruv heaved a deep sigh before setting to reply to her. He knew what guilt felt like and wanted to absolve her of hers.

Vratika,

I am alive, to say the least. Don't worry about me.

Don't blame yourself for Aamir's accident. You didn't do anything...the terrorists did.

You can absolve yourself of guilt for his accident. However, I don't think we can get back together again. I'm sorry if this sounds rude, but you and I should have broken up a long time ago.

Dhruv

After reading and replying to his e-mails for a few more minutes, he tried calling Sachi. Every time, the call went unanswered. It hurt him to see her lack of response. But then, he thought, she might be sleeping or busy. So he sent her a message: *'It's just been a day and I am missing you a lot already. Take care! – Dhruv'*

When he was done writing it, he got up and stretched, began to read the newspaper to pass time, prepared himself another cup of tea, and kept on calling and messaging Sachi. He received no responses to his phone calls or messages, which surprised him. He didn't want to think negative thoughts, but he felt she was making it obvious that she wanted to avoid him. And then he wondered: If she wanted to avoid him, why was she teary-eyed when they parted? Why was she as numb as the dead? He had a lot to think about. There was still something that he could not control. He was at a point in his life when he did not know what destiny held in store for him. Was there anything else he had that would be forcibly taken from him? He lay down on the sofa, and slept as soon as he closed his eyes.

Life went on, but he missed the sight of that one sensible face that could understand him better than anybody else cared to. He recalled how Mithun had come to see him at home, to check if he was okay. He missed Mithun and then remembered the discussion he had with him last night.

When he woke up, it was already dark. He saw Mithun's message on his mobile; it read:

'Hope you're doing okay, Tried calling you several times. Revert whenever you see this.'

When he saw this message, he called up Mithun. He smiled when he heard Mithun's voice and said, 'How are you, Mithun? I am so sorry I couldn't call you up earlier. I just got back today.'

'That's OK, Dhruv. Hope you're doing well,' he said.

Dhruv sensed something in his voice. 'Are you crying, Mithun? What happened?'

'Dhruv, I am at the hospital and my brother is dying, He's been on the dialysis machine for a long time. There have been so many serious issues regarding his health in the last fifteen days. I'm really worried. I can't bear to see my brother dying in front of my eyes.' Mithun was crying hysterically and kept repeating the same words again and again.

'Mithun, relax! Everything will be fine, we'll save him. Which hospital are you in? I'm coming to meet you,' he said.

'Bombay Hospital.'

'I will reach there as soon as I can. Till then, take care of yourself,' he said and disconnected the call.

Dhruv called Mithun as soon as he reached the hospital; Mithun came down to receive Dhruv and said nothing when they met. He was not the same man who had spoken of strength a month ago. He looked low, his body language reeked of disappointment and he seemed lost. As Dhruv hugged him, he began to weep and held him tight; it was the cry of a man who had held tears within himself for a long time. Dhruv didn't stop him; he knew Mithun needed to vent his emotions for him to be strong again.

He said, 'My brother is still on dialysis. The frequency has increased, keeping his critical condition in mind. He's dying day by day and I cannot save him.'

'What does the doctor say?' Dhruv asked, his hand on Mithun's shoulder, as they sat in the parking area.

'His kidneys have stopped functioning completely. They're just not sure of anything now. They've asked us for a kidney donation some days ago.'

'I think that's a hopeful sign. I've seen people live their life normally on one kidney. What's the problem?'

'My mother is too old to give it and I am diabetic; they don't accept kidneys from a diabetic patient. There's no other way out, Dhruv. There are still too many questions for which I have no answers. We're just waiting from one day to the next to find a solution, but we can't do anything…other than see him die.' He had lost all hope of saving his brother.

He had this uneasy feeling of losing somebody again. He had endured it recently and he did not want anyone else to endure so much pain in their lives. He could sense Mithun's fear as he listened to him sob. He could sense the heaviness in Mithun's heart as he spoke of Shantanu. This had been the most difficult time for Mithun; he didn't know what to say, what to do and what to expect from the future. Dhruv recalled how he had felt when Aamir had died; he would have done anything to see him alive and well at that moment.

'Do you think anybody else can donate a kidney to your brother?' He said as breathed in deeply.

'It's illegal unless someone does it of their own accord. But there's no use thinking of that; nobody would agree to it. Moreover, it's very difficult to get the right match and we don't have much time left.'

'I'll do it,' Dhruv said, and his voice was unusually serious.

'What? That's not funny, Dhruv. Do you even know what are you talking about? It's a kidney and it changes one's life,' Mithun said.

'Mithun, I wouldn't joke at such a critical time. I am serious when I say that I'll donate it. You talk to your doctors and let me know what needs to be done.'

There was silence for some time; something about the way he said it was totally unexpected.

'No, Dhruv. I can't let you do that. This is too much to ask for.'

'Can you let your brother die? Answer me!' he said, and a pained silence followed. 'Mithun, don't say no to this. It might work out for your brother and can give his life a new start. I've lost my brother. I can't let it happen again. We'll do everything possible to save your brother. I'll feel as if I've saved my brother and it will pacify my soul. Remember you only told me it's good to accept help sometimes, even from strangers.'

'It's not that easy to do. There are lots of tests that you need to go through. Your kidney should be accepted by his body. Since you are not a member of my family, there are fewer chances of it getting accepted.'

'It's still better than losing hope. We can at least get the kidney compatibility tests done. The rest will follow depending on the result.'

'Dhruv, you have your whole career ahead of you. It's much easier said than done. Think it over for yourself. What of your life ahead?'

'Mithun, even if I die during this operation and save your brother's life, I would be the happiest of men. And I've nobody left to live this life for anyway. Since you are a family man, you should be mature and understand the need of the hour. We shouldn't waste time. Stop being an idiot and start doing the needful please.'

'I don't know how much this will help him, but I really appreciate the concern and care you've shown, Dhruv. You've given me new hope,' Mithun said, and folded his hands before Dhruv.

'Don't say that! Now please get information on the details and tell me when I should get all the tests done.'

'I'll certainly do that, Dhruv. I'll just go to the doctor and check up on the details. I'll inform you as soon as possible.'

'And please think positive. I am hopeful that we'll save him. He's like a brother to me and you're my family.'

'You're a beautiful human being, Dhruv. Thank you so much, thanks for everything!' he said, hugging him tearfully.

'See you soon. Take care!' Dhruv said and waved his hand as he started towards his car.

As he left, he was pleased with what he had done. He remembered Aamir and prayed that all would be well. He had never felt so proud before. He felt he was giving Aamir a new lease of life. The fact that if everything worked out well, it would give life to somebody pleased him no end. He smiled and kept driving, thinking about his conversation with his father in Brahmi and what Sachi must be doing at this time.

20 August 2006

Mithun stood outside the Kidney Transplant Unit with very perplexing thoughts and emotions. He was surrounded by his family, all of whom looked hopeful and concerned. He couldn't figure out why Dhruv had answered his call. He couldn't figure out why Dhruv had agreed to come down for the tests in the blink of an eye. Didn't Dhruv know this would be a big deal? Didn't he know his life would change completely? He wouldn't again be able to play contact and adventure sports.

All his family members, who'd spent many sleepless nights with him, were now clinging to hope, with Dhruv's decision to donate a kidney to Shantanu. He glanced at the clock impatiently. He felt as if time was running out, yet standing still. Two lives were at stake – the life of someone he loved the most, and that of someone he respected the most. He was having a hard time accepting the reality of what was happening. Dhruv's words rang in his ears, all powerful and positive, 'Do not think much. You are a brave man; act like one. Everything's going to be fine.'

He was indebted to Dhruv for several lifetimes. He couldn't think of a way he could ever return the favour. When

Dhruv's blood group matched that of his brother, Mithun still wondered why Dhruv was making this sacrifice, even as he felt glad that things were working out. After all, it was what he had wanted most.

Mithun stared at the door of the operating theatre. Although the curtain over the glass window on the door was drawn, he could see the shadowy figures of doctors moving inside. He went to his mother and offered her a glass of water. She rejected it without looking at him. After all, it was her son inside, fighting a battle for his life. She had her eyes closed and fervently chanted God's name. She had been very strong all along. Shantanu had been on dialysis for some years, but she never missed a single session of it. She always made sure she was there to sit next to him. She sold her jewellery and her property; she did everything she could just to buy some more time for her son.

He then remembered the families, whose close relatives had been operated some days ago. He recalled every detail of their anxiety, behaviour and happiness when the operations were successful, though his heart broke for an eight-year-old child who had his kidney transplanted. He questioned God again about his cruelty to such a young child. He just hoped that anybody who came there never had to return empty-handed.

15 August 2006

After a series of tests, Mithun's family waited impatiently outside the laboratory for the results. Mithun went over to Dhruv, hugged him and said, 'You have taken God's place for us. I still don't understand why you have to do this for me. If anything goes wrong with you, I'll never be able to forgive myself.'

'Mithun, that won't happen. Trust me, we'll come out safely. I bet we'll be finished with the operation within a few hours and then you'll see us smiling again. Secondly, I am not doing this for you or anybody. I am doing it for a boy who's on the verge of life and death and there's no other alternative available to save him. I can't see another person dying in front of my eyes. Moreover, if Aamir was in your brother's place, I would've done the same thing for him. Then why do I have to think twice when it's Shantanu? I don't want to lead the same life again. I don't want myself to grow old as Dhruv, but as Aamir, who is a very compassionate person. I am sure Aamir would be proud of me now.'

'But what about work? Don't you think it's going to be difficult for you to take some more leave after a month off from office?'

'I've already decided to resign, Mithun. I will just visit our office a day before my operation for some time and do the rest of formalities. To be honest, I'm not certain I'd like to take up a job anytime soon.'

Mithun tried to talk some sense into Dhruv for not giving up on work just like that. That was the time when he needed money. He could not afford the luxury of not working. But Dhruv was adamant. He had just realized that life had no guarantees. He didn't want to die without living the dreams of his family. Although he knew there was nothing left in Brahmi, he wanted to try to live there. He did not know how he would do that, but he wanted to try. He knew there were people who would support him.

He smiled and put his hand on Mithun's shoulder. There was a lot on his mind, about the results, about the operation and its effects, about Aamir and Anvi. But they did not discuss it. They saw Dr. Laddha waving them into his cabin. As they entered, both of them felt nervous as the doctor asked them to sit.

'Look, I have got the test results,' Dr. Laddha said.

'What do they indicate?' Mithun asked anxiously as he leant forward.

'I haven't seen many such cases in which all the tests are so compatible. Fortunately, it's good news. But yes, everything depends upon this last test that we're left with. It's a kidney compatibility test. That basically checks if one can donate a kidney to the patient or not. It also reveals which kidney would suit our needs the best.'

Mithun and Dhruv looked relieved as if half the battle was already won. They both felt happy. They had been worried ever since the doctor spoke of kidney replacement, but the positive tests gave them hope.

'Thanks Doctor,' Mithun said.

'You should now get the last test done as soon as possible. Go to the reception, make the required payment, undergo the test and we'll soon receive the reports. I am hopeful. Best of luck.' The doctor smiled and waved them out. Both of them left feeling hopeful. This was the last test; all they wanted was to go back to a normal life, their hope and zest renewed.

Dhruv underwent the test. The reports were awaited. Dhruv left for his flat while Mithun went to fetch some medicines.

❀

20 August 2006

After half an hour, Mithun got up from his seat again to check if the operation was still going on. Yes, it was. They were all growing more and more tense with each minute that passed. Those moments were intense, terrifying. The stakes were high. No one was prepared for any adverse result.

17 August 2006

Dhruv went home and bathed. When he went to the cupboard to take out his clothes, he saw a greeting card lying at the back. As he opened it, he noticed that Aamir had made that greeting card himself, including the cutting and colouring. He smiled as he read those beautiful lines that he had written for Anvi.

To the girl who is adorable, cute and beautiful in her heart. Reasons to like you, adore you – never stop to last.

You're one fairy on this planet called earth. Your eyes, your smile, that's where I have my new world.

Talking to you never makes me bored; you're the breezy wind on the beautiful seashore.

Heaven on earth I wasn't aware, you rule my heart, and my love is in the air.

Whenever you need me, you'll always find me around. No matter the distance. It just doesn't count.

May you get all my happiness and I your sadness; You have a magical smile, no tears will I let you shed.

I sometimes wonder, if you're for real. Because, if I had any choice I would choose you over the entire world.

How lucky I am to have you in my life, you're a wonderful person with a mischievous glow in your eyes.

With you, forever isn't that long; I've my heart beating for you. Clear, sound and strong.

This beautiful feeling lights my undying love.

Many of them, come and go. You're one in all above.

Your laughter is like bubbles of energy; it makes the moment bright, sparkling and happy.

Lovely words that fall out from your lips; they're diamonds, the most precious gift.

That's a special feeling, a special desire. I love you to the moon and back. I am not a liar!! :)

To the girl who is adorable and beautiful in her heart. Reasons to like you, adore you – never stop to last.

You're one fairy on this planet called Earth. Your eyes, your smile, that's where I have my new world.

Aamir

He was breathless as he finished reading it. He realized with a pang that he was so obsessed with his own pain, he had almost forgotten about the lady who meant most to his brother. Now it was his responsibility to find Anvi and make sure she was doing well in her life. He decided to search for her.

On the other hand, he missed Sachi after reading his brother's card to Anvi. Before he dozed off, he called her thrice, hoping she would respond this time. But she did not answer his call. He thought she'd never talk to him as she might have been offended when he proposed to her. He slept on the couch and prayed for a better life ahead.

He slept peacefully after many days, hoping everything would turn out well for him, and also for Mithun and his family. He knew he'd not only save Shantanu's life, but in doing so would also make his own brother very proud. His dreams were interrupted by a message on his mobile which said:

'This isn't less than a miracle. I am so happy to tell you that your left kidney is compatible with Shantanu's kidney. You came across as an angel in our lives. Now that you've shown us this way out, I promise that I'll stay positive and will be there for whatever you need in your life. I saw my mother smile for the first time in the past few months. I called you up to inform you about this, but you must be sleeping. There are certain formalities which need to be finished soon. See you tomorrow and I'll tell you everything. Love you. Smile all the way.'

Dhruv smiled after reading the message and thought of the happy faces in the hospital, including Shantanu's. He lay there, looking at Aamir's portrait in the living room, thinking that he was finally giving life back to Aamir in some other form. He dialled the same helpline number that he had called many times before. Unfortunately, he got no hopeful response yet again. His mind filled with thoughts and hopes and plans, he closed his eyes again and slept peacefully.

20 August 2006

Mithun went to have some water, checking his watch every few minutes. He realized the operation had taken four hours and it would end soon. But those last few minutes were definitely the toughest and slowest of his life. He couldn't wait to see Shantanu set free of the tormenting pain.

17 August 2006

After the Man Social Welfare (MSW) formalities of data collection and address verification had been done, they sent an application to the hospital for verification. After that, it didn't take long for a board meeting in the hospital along with the donor, the patient and their relatives, to find out if the donor was donating his kidney of his own volition. After the formalities were completed, the doctor scheduled the operation, informing the patient, his family and the donor. The operation would take place within three days; Dhruv was to get admission two days before.

'I can't imagine myself wearing such horrible clothes. Could somebody please tell them I am not a patient? The patient is somebody else!' Dhruv said, faking an indignant tone.

'No, I've ordered a Louis Vuitton suit for you. You'll not get operated till you wear the suit.' Mithun laughed.

'Thank you for making fun of me! Doctors, I tell you! Why can't they just take my kidney out and let me leave? It's so simple. Why make it complicated?'

'I am telling you, open all the records from the past of this hospital and they wouldn't have got such an entertaining inmate in a long time. Believe me!'

Dhruv gave him a funny look. 'I am cursing you, Mithun. May you marry Rubeena and have the ugliest kids in the world.'

'You fucker! Wait, I'll tell the doctor to not give you any good food.'

Both of them rolled with laughter. It was definitely not a moment to be laughed about, but all those jokes made all the difference and eased their painful journey. They kept negative vibes and thoughts away till the time came for the kidney transplant.

20 August 2006

After what seemed like a million lifetimes had passed, their anxious wait came to an end. The doors of the operation theatre were thrown open and one by one the doctors started coming out. Mithun and his family rose to their feet. Their hearts felt as if they were going to explode any moment. When they saw Dr. Laddha emerging out of the room, everyone's facial expressions tightened. The talk in the waiting room fell to an eerie silence. The moment was killing. The doctor remained silent for a few seconds. Everyone was restlessly waiting for him to speak and deliver the news.

20 August 2006 (Morning)

Mithun sat close to Dhruv and held his hand. Their minds were racing in hundreds of directions, but none of them said anything. It was Dhruv who spoke first, 'I don't know what to say, Mithun. But you need to be strong all this while and keep Shantanu strong too. He needs you more than me. Trust me, it's just a matter of a few hours and everything will be fine.' As he said this, his voice was soft and he smiled at him.

Mithun was looking down at him, grateful and teary-eyed as he didn't know what would happen in a few hours. It might be two different extremes. It might make their lives or break their lives, for obvious reasons.

Dhruv spoke of Anvi and Aamir to Mithun as he also explained Brahmi's incident and his unexpected interaction with his father in his dream. He asked him to run a check on Aamir and Anvi, to find out if she was doing okay in case things did not turn out well. Mithun broke into a cold sweat after listening to everything and scolded Dhruv for not telling him anything before. 'You wouldn't have allowed me to do the donation then, and both you and me know how urgent it is.' He smiled and replied.

'Come back soon, we're waiting outside and don't you worry about anything, Dhruv. You've been so good for me, this is the least I can do for you,' Mithun said, smiled and hugged him for one last time before the operation and went to Shantanu's room.

'I love you, Shantanu. Just be strong and you will be back… fit and fine.' That was one moment for which they were really scared and most hopeful.

'Are you scared?' Shantanu asked.

'No, I am not.' Mithun said without making eye contact.

'Yes, you are. I can see it. You are allowed to be a little worried, but not scared. We have come this far, and we are now finally going to make it through. This is all going to end well.' Mithun's eyes shone with pride at his little brother's courage. He kissed him on the forehead and made room for his mother to see Shantanu. She also blessed him and Shantanu assured them in return. Soon, the doctor signalled the ward boys to take Shantanu to the transplant room.

Both Dhruv and Shantanu were taken to the transplant room together. Before going inside, they both waved cheerfully at everyone outside and imagined what it would be like to emerge out of that room all cured.

'You can stand outside and we'll inform you as soon as the operation gets over. We all hope for the best,' Dr. Laddha said and entered the transplant room. His words meant a lot to everybody at that moment.

❀

20 August 2006 (Noon)

After some seconds, he smiled and said, 'Many congratulations. Everything went well. The kidney has been accepted and Shantanu responded well. Both of them are healthy and fine. Dhruv will be discharged after three days from the ICCU and Shantanu will be discharged after twenty days. We'll keep on updating you about their health. Time for some sweets and celebrations! In fact, I'll have one as well.'

Everyone first froze at the words. They didn't know how to respond. As the meaning of the doctor's words finally sunk in, they jumped up in joy. Suddenly, their broken world was brought together, all fixed. It was a miracle. They had never been happier in their lives. They shouted and cried and hugged each other like never before, as if getting rid of the tensions they'd experienced in the past few months. Mithun fell on his knees and touched the doctor's feet. They were calling out Dhruv's name – he was the one person who had made it possible; they were thanking and blessing him. Mithun went on to hug his mother who was crying in sheer happiness.

Everyone then turned to the doctor who was simply standing there, looking at them in this emotional state. 'Doctor, there are no words in the world that I could put together to thank you.' Mithun was finding it very hard to even speak.

'It was my duty, Mithun. I will write down some medications that you need to get and also there are certain precautions that need to be taken. But yes, I'd like to say, cases like this reinforce my faith in the existence of God. Congratulations once again.' He gave a firm smile and walked away, leaving them to soak in the moment of happiness.

It felt amazing that they had survived, as they had nearly lost him a couple of times before. Yes, miracles happen. But only for those who put their faith in it.

The last few days had been the best as both of them were recovering well. After a week, Dhruv was to be discharged from the ICCU. He no longer made any effort to make Mithun smile as everyone had already got their smiles back. Mithun brought some nice flowers and DVDs along with a beautiful framed photograph of Aamir, which he got made when Dhruv was resting in the ICCU.

However, Shantanu had to spend some more time in the hospital. He was recovering fast and the kidney was responding really well. Mithun went back to work and made Dhruv promise that they would eat together every day and visit each other every day after work. In Mithun's eyes, he was no longer just a friend, but a younger brother too. They were now three brothers in one family. Dhruv was extremely happy to be a part of their family.

He reminded himself that he had a lot of things to take care of. The first thing was to find Anvi. After that, he could take decisions regarding his future and career. He was also dying to talk to Sachi. He decided to give it another try by calling her in case she finally responded. He had missed her terribly over the last few days and he would trade his soul to be with her for one more time. He imagined what it would be like if she were around that time, taking care of him, and inspiring him.

Finally, the doctor signed Dhruv's discharge certificate. Dhruv walked out of the hospital content and smiling.

19 August 2006

He dressed for work. He looked much better now than he had last month. He'd brushed his hair, shaved off the stubble on his face and wore Aamir's white shirt, which had come in from the laundry. Aamir often told him they looked alike when they both wore white on the same day. The thought itself made him smile.

He was returning to work after a month. He parked his car and rode up in the elevator to his office on the third floor. He noticed that his colleagues from the other departments were standing around, whispering about the reason for his sudden decision to take leave. He was not surprised by their behaviour; he had expected it.

However, his mind was on other things. He'd promised Aamir that he would not let him down, ever. He'd spent a lot of time thinking about what he wanted from life. As he entered the office, he smiled at Rubeena. It was strange for him to smile at someone who had never really cared for him, but just tortured him at work. However, when she walked up to him, she hugged him and said, 'Good to see you back, Dhruv. Welcome back.' He smiled again.

She was trying to be friendly and make him feel as comfortable as possible. She was certainly happy to see him back. 'I am so sorry for that mail. I am sure you needed time. But I had to send it because of company policy. You know how it is with our company; they need everything documented,' she said.

'I can understand,' he said. He wasn't certain if it was company policy or not. But he was not there to argue with her; he had other fish to fry. 'Rubeena, I want to talk to you about something.'

'Yes, Dhruv. Tell me, what is it about?' She looked puzzled as she spoke.

'Not here. Can we talk in your cabin?' he said.

'Sure. Come!' she said and led the way to her cabin.

'Rubeena, the past few days of my life have been most difficult for obvious reasons, but I've accepted my life the way it is now. I went back to my hometown for some time to get some peace of mind. Hence, I couldn't receive or reply to any mails. I apologize for behaving so unprofessionally. I was out of my mind with grief and wanted to get away for some time.'

'I don't think you need to worry, Dhruv. Now that you're back, I am sure we'll work that out. I spoke to the boss about you and convinced him to extend your leave. Just be careful when you meet him and everything else is taken care of,' she said. She was talking softly; she had never behaved so kindly before and had always been rather bitchy to him.

'No Rubeena, you don't understand. It's not about this job. I had no fear of losing it. In fact, I think I'll never be able to work here in the same way ever again. I think it's time I moved on in my personal and professional life. It's what I need to do now. I've decided to resign.' He spoke softly as he handed over his resignation letter to her.

The cabin was much warmer than it had been some minutes ago. Dhruv had never spoken of a resignation in the past several years. He had frequently been awarded as a top performer. This sudden resignation was totally unexpected. Rubeena looked as shocked and worried as she had looked excited to see Dhruv walk back into the office a few minutes back. She knew Dhruv's qualities and qualification were all that the company needed in its employees.

There was silence for some time before Rubeena asked, 'Why the sudden decision, Dhruv? You've been working very well for a long time. I'm sure you just need some time and you'll be back with a bang. This is when you need this job the most and you're talking about quitting. Don't take a decision at this time of emotional turmoil. Think it over; sleep over it. I can't accept your resignation.'

'Rubeena, I've thought a lot about it and I don't think there's any more thinking I can do. I can't pretend to work and then be lost somewhere else. It just doesn't sound fair to me. I need this break from life at the moment to figure out what I should do in future. I'm not taking this decision emotionally and I'm sure there will be some way out for me. Perhaps this is the best for me.' He spoke every word as if it came from the heart.

'I could talk to the boss if you insist, but I am sure he'll want to negotiate it with you to find a possible way out. But do you think this is a sensible decision at all, Dhruv? If you want my opinion, I still don't consider it the best decision. It might give you inner satisfaction at first, but the world doesn't work like that. I too faced a similar situation when my father died. But I promised myself to be brave and move on. In hindsight, I took the best decision for myself. In all honesty, Dhruv, I don't think anybody else would care and they'll forget you like any other employee after you resign. But ask yourself if you're making the right decision for yourself? I really hope you don't think later that you've been a fool to leave a job like this when you needed it the most. All in all, your decision doesn't sound too good to me.'

'Thanks for your concern, Rubeena. But you can be certain that you will never find me in such a situation in my life. I am still young enough to start a new life. Plus, I have a lot of unfinished work to do, and I guess it's time I completed them.'

'Well, if you've already taken this decision and think that it's good enough for you, you leave me with no choice. I really feel bad accepting your resignation. You have always been an outstanding performer and team player, and an amazing human being who always made people laugh. I cannot think of an instance in the past when you gave up on a challenge. I'll be glad to work with you any time in the future. You will always find our door open. You deserve lots and lots of happiness in life,' she said. She felt genuinely bad at losing such a star performer, who was also a thorough gentleman at the workplace. He was somebody she could rely upon.

He was certainly aware of what he was doing. He knew he had to find a new way to live his life now. It wasn't as easy for him as he made it out to be. But he didn't want to hang on here. He felt he would never be at peace if he stayed on here; he would be in the same state he had been in some months ago.

'Thanks very much, Rubeena. When I think of my time here, I think of how much I've learnt, of how much I've grown here as a person. It's been a pleasure working with you too. And trust me, I never really thought that I would feel bad resigning. But yes, I am being emotional because I have been here for the past three years. It was a second home to me.'

Immediately, Rubeena got up, hugged him and said, 'We'll do a fantastic farewell party for you; would you mind?'

'No, not at all. It's high time my company paid me back for all the effort I've put in,' he said and smiled.

'I'll ensure that.' As she said that, they walked out of her cabin and saw the business head, Danny standing there and looking at Dhruv. He had a couple of newspapers in his hands. He had a charming personality and looked intelligent. He was much esteemed in the office and from a socially respectable background.

'Attention everybody, There's something I want to tell all of you here.' As he spoke, every face in the room turned towards him and everything became very serious within a minute. His voice was that of a man who controlled this office. All this while, Dhruv kept thinking of what had happened.

'Well, I've one habit that I follow daily, and I don't change my habits so quickly. I read the newspapers every day,' he said. 'So, I was reading the newspapers this morning as always and I almost turned to ice after reading an opinion piece. It described someone's feelings very realistically and honestly. I'm grateful to the media for publishing such a brilliant eye opener. But I truly respect someone who faced a difficult time last month and still had the courage to give it in the face to everyone. Hats off to you, Dhruv. You're there in all the papers.' He bowed as he said this.

'Can I read this, sir?' Dhruv asked and Danny gave him all the newspapers he had been holding in his hands. As he read each paper, he noticed that they had all printed his open letter on the front page, with his name.

'You are right to say that we have got used to things and we should all be blamed for it, Dhruv. We are so caught up in our personal lives that we do not care about our own people and find different ways to shirk responsibility. To be honest, I've been one such person. I have been lucky not to endure what you have been through last month. Things have changed a lot for you, Dhruv, and we know that. We admire you and are always there for you in whatever you need. The least I can do is to promise you that I'll never be an insensitive person, as I have been in the past. I'll fight against every wrong in this country,' Danny said as he believed that every word of Dhruv's letter made sense.

He was grateful that the media had published his open letter that he had written on his blog, along with a picture of him and Aamir. Danny had acknowledged it at work, in front of his colleagues. He'd begun a struggle that was his right to wage. His colleagues expressed their pride in and sympathy for him; they applauded what he had done after Danny finished speaking. Everybody hugged him to ensure him that he was not alone.

Dhruv cast one last glance at the letter he had penned a couple of nights back. The pain in his heart had taken the form of words; it had been picked up by media houses, even made viral on medial platforms across the city and nation.

> *I am Dhruv, one of those lucky bastards who is still breathing, I am grateful to many people for this. Terrorists and politicians are at the top of my list. Although no thank you is big enough to describe what you have done for me, I am still trying to put it into words.*

First of all, I would like to thank the terrorists for not killing me while performing their latest atrocity and allowing me to breathe for some more days, which is such a fortunate thing to talk about. You certainly have taken away many talented people, who could have competed against me professionally. And you have reduced the Indian population with your random killings; we can now breathe deeply. It does not matter if our breath is that of fear or anger. To most of us, it makes no difference. You have forced us to realise that this is not just a dog-eat-dog world, but a human-eat-human world also. We now have a few more historical monuments to show tourists – the memorials in aftermath of terrorist atrocities.

Now you've given us something else to argue about – which was the bigger attack, the bombs on the train or the bombs in the middle of a crowded market? But that's not a big issue; I'm sure the statisticians will sort it out. Such an exciting activity, isn't it? We say cricket is the most popular sport here, but I disagree, because I think terrorism is more popular than cricket. And like the best of sportsmen, you play with the lives of millions. That requires lots of dedication and effort.

Unlike doctors, who have added years to our lives by getting rid of serious diseases such as tuberculosis and smallpox, your bombs and bullets end lives, not discriminating in favour of anyone on the basis of age. Whereas we speak of equality and non-discrimination on the basis of caste, religion or state, you put it into practice. You've left no part of our country unscathed. And please don't think I am complaining. No, not at all! You rule this country. How dare I even think about it? We love you, which is why we keep allowing you to do things that you want. I am sometimes really lost for words when I start appreciating all that you have done for us.

In fact, we should do some time management lectures with you as an example, so that our grads learn something from you. Come on, planting five bombs and blasting all of them in ten minutes – can there be a better example of time management and punctuality than this? I guess not. And don't worry about your friends here; they're safe and secure. Carefully looked after. You wouldn't be disappointed in our hospitality. You can ask your friends who're still enjoying our hospitality for the past so many decades. You rule our heart, because you play well with it.

I'm still not complaining about anything. You're always welcome. I hope we always bond as well as we do now, and you permit me to live, as always. If it had not been for you, we wouldn't have respected relations as much as we do now. There's a lot left to say, but I really need to keep it brief since we're not in the habit of reading something long and meandering. So, I thank you once more for playing with our emotions, life and family as you have always done.

Last, but definitely not the least, I would like to thank our politicians for being ever so calm and composed while playing effortless politics. You too rule this country. Whatever I say about you would be less than what you actually deserve. We're grateful to have you, since you all have magical powers. You can get criminals, who actually killed members of our family directly or indirectly, to stand for elections. You also ensure that India's reputation for hospitality does not suffer when you give all sorts of luxuries to terrorists. You're so professional that every time a terrorist attack takes place, you forget that we're Indians first and professionals second...when with all your heart, soul and mind you curse the party in power and hold them responsible rather than supporting security in our country. This says a lot about your dedication to your nation.

I'm always amazed at your confidence. When it's time for elections, you talk about security first and everything else later on. But when it comes to actual implementation, security is unavailable and there's no awareness on that subject. But you would certainly have a logical reason for doing what you do. You can make a living person die and bring back the dead to life. You still say that you will not let the culprits go after every terrorist act and give them warning. For all your love for the country and its people, you cannot use violence to defeat the enemies, no matter how many innocent Indians perish. I'm sure you have your reasons for acting the way you do. And we need to tolerate that because we elected you to office for a certain period of time. We have also learnt how to maximize our utilization of resources from you. We pay taxes, expecting our basic needs will be met. However, we are still burdened with more taxes, which we pay when we visit cafés and restaurants, but we do not enjoy security. You are certainly using us as a resource to be utilized to the maximum. You certainly know how to press our emotional buttons. You have seldom made us happy.

It's not everybody's cup of tea to play politics with the dead, which you manage to do quite successfully, Everything bad that happens in our country, which hurts peoples' emotions in the worst possible way is a part of politics, and that's the most frequently played game by you.

For all the love you've given to me till date, I promise not to expect anything from you. No security, no good treatment, no happiness and above all, no freedom in our independent country, because with all your combined direct or indirect effort, you've hurt me too…with this maximum strike. Thank you so much!

I'm not sure what I'll do with this after I finish writing it. But I'm writing this letter to everybody who claims to have emotions, gets hurt, loves their family and gets disappointed at times.

My brother Aamir is missing after the terrorist attacks last month; he was one amongst the hundreds injured there. But if you ask me what keeps me going, I will say that it is my brother who keeps me going. He is with me whenever I need him. A missing man is a support, while a living man is a threat.

Your Victim,
Dhruv

19 August 2006 (Evening)

He was surprised to arrive at his flat within a few minutes. There hadn't been any traffic. He was mesmerized by the fact that he'd do a kidney donation to save somebody's life which resultantly would make Aamir proud. But this was not all he wanted to think about; he'd promised his father more than this. He knew that the time had come to make plans in detail. Trying to re-search for Aamir was one of them after he came out of hospital. Though he had resumed his search for Aamir as soon as he reached Mumbai, unfortunately, he had got no positive results. He decided to follow his instincts and help Shantanu with an urgent kidney donation.

It was late at night and he had to go back to the hospital for a big operation tomorrow. He put away the things that were no longer useful and saw many things that had belonged to Aamir, so he treasured them. It was then that he saw a beautiful diary made of the same feather paper that he had seen at his home in Brahmi. He couldn't take his eyes off it.

To be honest, he had no idea what it was. He was surprised to see it. It was Aamir's diary. He became curious beyond limit, and began reading it. Aamir began by describing their life in Mumbai, where they had come after their parents' deaths. As he read, he realised that he had learnt much about his childhood since his journey to Brahmi. He kept on reading and didn't stop for a single second. He smiled, looked serious and concerned after reading of his childhood with Aamir.

Then he was amazed when he read about Anvi and Aamir. It was such a hurtful feeling for him that he had no idea about his brothers' love life or that he never really showed much interest in it. It was the purest form of love between the couple. It was amazing to read how they met, the moments they shared, their love, their plans and their struggles. He started respecting Anvi and Aamir even more and was ashamed of himself after finding out that he was the reason why Aamir never got married to Anvi. Aamir feared that Dhruv would feel insecure, because that was his nature. Aamir's love was such that he sacrificed his own happiness for his younger brother, who had never really bothered to discuss his love life. It was certainly the same person who wrote this diary who was so much in love with a woman that he could go beyond life to please her, and yet again it was the same person who wrote this diary who had gone beyond all limits to see his younger brother happy.

There was something that he read which shocked him. Dhruv never really knew the climax of this love story before he read this.

Anvi Sharma, how wonderful that day was when we met first, fell in love, kissed for the first time and shared so many memories. Believe me, when I spoke to you first, I knew I'll fall in love as soon as I looked into your eyes. I found my world in your eyes. Every time you talked, you were so charming. I remember everything that we shared. Our walks on the beach, our chats in the coffee shops, jogging in the park, occasional fights, dancing in the rain...in fact everything in the world is priceless. These past few years with you were indeed priceless.

Do you remember when we first talked about Brahmi? Wasn't that just a wonderful place? I still remember how you loved it and asked me if we were still on the same planet. I could see in your eyes that you wanted to be there for the rest of your life. I felt so close to my real self after so long. I really want to get married to you and settle there. But we had to drop that plan – for your work, for my work and for our life that still goes on the same way in Mumbai.

Above all, I really respect you for your passion for your work in journalism, your writing and your focus on getting your work published and recognized. I still remember how afraid I always was, keeping the risk of your career in mind. I got really scared after that terrorist attack in the crowded market where you were reporting. That day, I almost thought that I had lost you; it was too hard to believe. But by God's grace, you came back and you were fine. I was fighting tears that time too, for reasons known best to you. We both were certain that it would eventually work out and you would be all right. But, whatever happened, we both shouldn't forget the fact that we were so proud when you got an award for the best journalist. When you were smiling on the stage and you thanked me from the podium, all I wanted was to hug you. You were looking so very beautiful that night. Time passed on too fast after that.

I remember that day, it was eight-thirty in the evening when I called you and you didn't pick up my call for the next two hours. Knowing that you were on some secret mission against child molesters, it frightened me to no end. Those minutes were too difficult to endure. I called up your office, but they refused to tell me where you were and said you must be fine and you'll call me back soon. I felt it was too irresponsible of them to react like that. I was fighting back tears even thinking of what might have happened to you. I promised myself that even if it broke this relationship, I would not let you work as a reporter anymore. I waited for you to come and hug me, or at least make a simple call or message, conveying that everything is OK. And it didn't take long to get that call from you.

You were happy to have found relevant information about those criminals; you told me everything without even a pause. You were so happy that you promised me to shift into news anchoring if these criminals got caught, which you believed they would, soon.

And I promised to make you meet Dhruv *that night and prepare your favourite meal for dinner in that gathering.*

You agreed and sounded joyous and excited like never before. But then, suddenly, everything shattered by a series of gun shots that I heard over the call. It didn't take me a second to understand the bullet's target…I heard you scream. I shouted over the call; I was dying to hear if you're okay. And the next moment, you were on all news channels. Lying on the road, in a pool of your own blood.

I was about to explode out of sheer anxiety. By the time I reached the spot, you had been taken away to the hospital. It was hard for me to breathe.

I reached the hospital as soon as I could, my legs were moving of their own volition. I nearly went numb because of fear as I asked about you. The last thing I remembered before I fell unconscious was a doctor communicating to another. 'Thankfully we have saved her. But she's in deep coma. Her body isn't responding.'

As I got back to my senses, I saw your news on television again and they read it as if it was any other news item. They said a reporter had been shot just below her head in an ongoing sting operation and she's very serious, for which they feel sorry. They said you were in coma. They didn't even mention your name. I was numb, senseless and lost for the next few minutes. How can anybody in this world be so cruel? How can you be shot? You did no wrong to anybody.

You were so good at your work and you were confident of coming out soon. I had prepared your favourite food and we're yet to have that. No, this just can't be the truth, Anvi. We've planned all our life; we're yet to be married. I was about to talk to Dhruv about you in a few days. Your birthday is just after a couple of weeks, and we're going to celebrate it at the park where we've planted trees in memory of our parents. You just can't go away like this, Anvi. That's just so inhumane. I lost my parents at a young age. I just can't afford to lose you now. But yes, this was reality. You were everywhere on the news, Anvi. But you were lying dead with a breathing body. I lost myself with you. I had lost a lot of my life with you; my sense and my entire motive to live this life.

People come to me and say - It's all right, Aamir. Everything will be fine, you'll learn to live without her and she's nobody but a dead person lying, but who will make them understand that there are certain things that will always remain the same? My love for you can't fade away; my memories can't fade away either. I have felt far too much because of the incident. No matter what it takes, I'd wake you up one day. My love will win over all this hate and I'll come, sit next to you and talk to you hours and hours. I'll try and sense your breath if you can't speak.

I regret that I couldn't stop you that day. I regret that I couldn't stop you for one last time and tell you how much you mean to me. I regret that nobody in this world would ever be able to understand me, you or the sacrifice you've made for our nation.

Aamir

Dhruv was shaken after reading this. Knowing that Anvi was in coma came as a shock to him, but that was not enough. He read some more in which Aamir talked about his struggle with life and his desire to make Dhruv happy always. Then he read this entry in the diary under the date 11 July 2006.

I just sensed something really bad when I woke up. For the past few days, I get very negative vibes. It feels as if something terrible is going to happen. The feeling is strong and I can't ignore it. I feel as if somebody is grabbing me and Dhruv. But as I write this, my body is shivering. I saw a dream that Dhruv died in a terrible accident and he's bleeding and crying and has lost his mind before he reaches the hospital. I can't imagine it happening. I've lost many people in my life who were close to my heart. My heart sinks at the thought of anything terrible happening to him. I believe that death can't be postponed; it's just about the circumstances and time.

Just the thought of Dhruv driving my car in anger gave me jitters. I didn't want to upset him. But thank god he reached office safely. I think I made the right decision by opting to go give money to Vratika myself, as the dream I had was not a positive one for him. I'll go and do the needful and see him in Bandra today evening.

I don't know why and how, but I strongly feel that something terrible will happen very soon. I would not like Dhruv to be a part of it. God, if anything wrong happens, let it happen to me and not to Dhruv.

God, give us enough courage to face this time and so hope that my intuitions are wrong this time. I hope to see Dhruv this evening.

This diary had changed his ideas about his brother and his life. It was so hard for him to believe what he read, for it was not something he could forget. He wasn't hoping to read something like that when he started reading this diary. He was shaken to realise that Aamir sacrificed his life for him after getting such strong intuitions. He was incredibly stressed to know of the inhumane accident that happened with Anvi. He could not believe that Aamir hadn't shared such a big tragedy with him, even if to ease his pain and suffering. Was he so immature that his elder brother could not even open up to him? The thought pained him no end. But this wasn't a moment to question what Aamir had not done; this was a time to take control over things. He wanted to read more about the incident with Anvi, so he started searching for information on Anvi Sharma, journalist, online.

He got various results:

Anvi Sharma Journalism student

Anvi Sharma Awards

Anvi Sharma Shot on head during a sting operation

Anvi Sharma in coma

He sat there for sometime as his heartbeats sped up with every passing second. This tide of emotions and shock just didn't seem to be over yet. He was out of his mind, not prepared to believe what was happening around him. He wanted to disagree with what he had just seen, but he knew it was true. He had many questions, but no answers. This was excruciatingly painful news to him. He walked around, took out his mobile, thought about certain incidents in the past few days and lost every sense of the world. His soul felt like in torment. He felt more connected to Aamir and Anvi.

11 July 2006

It had happened again. This time it was the evening commuters in local trains of Mumbai. The bombs were set off in the pressure cookers on trains plying the western lines. Someone had once again set out to disrupt life and peace of the city. Nothing has been done on security grounds till now, and the heart of India, Mumbai was attacked brutally once again by terrorists. The nation, the authorities, the government and everyone who could have made a difference by being responsible, had failed at saving innocent people… this time too.

It was surprising that no police and rescue workers reached sooner. It was citizens who took responsibility of rescuing the victims. Media houses were showing it as 'Breaking News', and were busy announcing that they were the first ones to telecast it. The media had descended in full force, hungry for sound bites, pictures and video footage. This dastardly attack on Mumbai local claimed many lives and what remained were personal items strewn around, remains of train carriages, heaps of metal, destroyed infrastructure flowing with innocent blood. Those who had survived were in pain, stressed, angry and desperate for help, irrespective of where it came from.

Dr. Deshmukh was lucky enough to have gotten late to board a train that evening. He was still outside the station that had been partially cordoned off for the public. He saw victims being rushed for medical help. Not sure if the blasts had stopped, he wanted to reach the safety of his house sooner. He turned to go back home before it got worse, but somebody caught his eye – a victim who was bleeding and looked under shock. He continued to watch him as the victim walked helplessly, as if he had no idea if he'd ever be able to reach home. There was a real possibility that he'd not be able to reach the hospital by himself too. He hadn't been able to tolerate and believe this whole thing, perhaps. He was too depressed, shocked and lost. He had managed to walk out of the station after impact. As he walked some more, his vision got blurred and he fell in the middle of the street. Dr. Deshmukh ran towards him and held him in his arms. The man was hurt, and almost unconscious. Still, he kept on murmuring two names continuously – Anvi and Dhruv. He was sounding like a heartbroken child.

Deshmukh was a man in his mid-40s. He could have ignored all this completely and moved on to the safety of his home. But he wasn't as sure about the situation. To ignore it and move away didn't seem fair to him. Between all the shouts and terror there, he first thought of taking him to a public hospital nearby. But he saw a lot of vehicles carrying injured people to hospitals; he was sure the nearest hospitals would be teeming with thousands by now and this man in his arms would not get adequate attention. Contradicting his own thoughts, he decided to take him to his own small set-up of a hospital in Bandra. This man needed urgent treatment and personal attention. He played god's disciple and hired a taxi to take him there.

As soon as he reached, he asked his staff to do the needful. While giving him first aid, they saw he was bleeding at several points; the shrapnel had pierced his body. Dr. Deshmukh instructed the staff to take him to the operation theatre.

'Are you sure you want to do this?' his wife asked.

'I'm sure. I don't want somebody else to lose their son now,' he said. 'We're losing time. We need to save him...somehow, anyhow. You need to come with me,' he added. He convinced her to take care of this person. But deep down, she knew he was doing it for himself. Dr. Deshmukh still majorly regretted the day he couldn't save his own son's life after an accident.

No one walked into Deshmukh's cabin after the operation was over. He knew the situation too well. All this while, he had just wanted to save him and get some details about Aamir. After the terrible shock that Aamir has faced, his body got affected and went numb. He got a paralysis attack and even worse, faced a rare form of fear, which might or might not go away with time.

26 August 2006

The past month-and-a-half had been one of the toughest in his life. Not for once forgetting the fear that they had lived through, Dr. Deshmukh picked up his phone. His hands were trembling slightly. Then, taking a deep breath, he dialled the number.

'Hello.'

'Is this Dhruv?'

'Yes, who's this?'

'I'm sorry that I didn't call you earlier. But then, I thought it wasn't going to be any easier to understand what I say. Moreover, I got your contact details some days back from a newspaper article you had written.'

Dhruv thought it was someone who wanted to talk about his open letter that had been published a week back. Many had lost their loved ones, and he had been flooded with mails and comments on his blog.

He said, 'I'm still trying to make sense of it myself. Please tell me what you want to say, and who are you?'

'It's regarding your brother, Aamir.'

There was absolute silence for a while. Night had almost fallen, and he could hear the sound of his own breath as he asked this. 'Is he with you? Is he alive? Who are you? Please tell me.'

'I am Dr. Deshmukh. I'll tell you everything. He is with me, and uhh…is fine. It's a little difficult to explain it all over a phone call. But please come to my address. I am texting it to you right away, Dhruv.'

'Yes, I'll be there at the earliest possible. Please message.' He smiled and the unexplained tears had the hope of getting Aamir back.

'B-301, Suryakiran Apt, Nearby Carter road, Bandra (West). Please come. Waiting for you. Deshmukh.'

As soon as he received the text, he ran down the stairs and stepped in his car. And all this while, he kept his hopes intact.

After the operation, Dr. Deshmukh kept giving Aamir the necessary treatment to keep him active. After earnest consultation with other senior doctors, he kept him away from outside world activities, which would help him recover. It had been more than twenty days that he brought Aamir to his hospital. He had Aamir's responsibility for long enough, hence he dedicated all his days and nights to make his health steady. The shock had pushed Aamir into temporary amnesia; he didn't remember a thing. He just chanted Anvi's and Dhruv's name like a medicine. Dr. Deshmukh tried to get his memory back. He felt more like a worried father than an over-worked doctor.

Dhruv drove like a crazy person all his way from Andheri to Bandra. He knew he was breaking traffic rules, but much was at stake. Traffic cops tried catching him at a couple of occasions, but were helpless in the face of his need. He was out of his own senses after that call. He finally reached the mentioned address and pushed the doorbell of the house. He wanted to get in immediately and desperately. He had myriad hopes, and feared somewhere in his mind that none of them would come true.

Somebody opened the door and asked him to come in. He could hear Deshmukh talking to someone, and on silent feet he walked up to him and opened the door. He glanced at him with a smile. He said not even a single word and just sat down there.

'It's so good to see you, Dhruv,' Deshmukh said and Dhruv thanked him back. Deshmukh could see the hope in Dhruv's eyes. 'Are you alright?' he asked Dhruv.

'Yes, I am. Please tell me why you called me here.' He said this with a strange wistful look in his eyes, as if he was almost begging for information on Aamir. He had never been so nervous and desperate in his life before.

'As I said, it's regarding your brother Aamir. I read your article in a newspaper along with a picture of you both. Since then, I've been trying to call you, but your number was switched off. But thankfully, your call got connected today and we talked. I met Aamir after that attack, He was bleeding a lot and he suddenly got off his senses. I decided to bring him to my own hospital and give him proper treatment. So much had happened that day, and it leaves me scared to even think about what all has happened in the last twenty odd days, Dhruv. He has gone through a paralysis attack and also lost a part of his memory in those terrorist attacks. He has gone through a lot, but it's no less than a miracle to see his will power to survive again and fight again. I feel wonderful to say that…'

'They saved me, Dhruv.' Somebody said it from behind him, smiling at him from a distance. Dhruv knew the voice even before he turned around. Aamir made no move to come towards him. He was weak, pale and more fragile now.

Dhruv was teary-eyed as he turned around to see him. He couldn't believe it. His eyes were wide. It was Aamir's voice. Aamir was alive.

For a moment, everything around him faded, except the voice of Aamir and his face.

As soon as Dhruv smiled and stood up to hug him, he felt blank. Getting there was taking a long time. As he reached for him, he was practically hyperventilating. He kneeled down, screamed and looked absolutely exhausted. He broke down. He had been so brave all this while. When Aamir left, he had no idea whether he'd able to see his brother ever again in his life. It had been a long time. He was dying to hear him, to see him smiling, or just hug him tightly. Dhruv was a tough guy after everything that he had gone through, but he was crying so hard that his face hurt. He had scarcely talked to anybody about anything else after Aamir's incident. It was undoubtedly the happiest moment of his life. And in the distance, behind them, was a happy father – Dr. Deshmukh, smiling with tears.

'I am sorry, Dhruv. It took me so long to come back. I can understand what you've gone through. But I wasn't even in a position to speak,' Aamir said, as he picked him up and tears welled in his eyes as he hugged him.

'I'm just glad you're alive, Aamir. My intuitions were right; you are back. I searched for you in hospitals, called helpline numbers hundreds of times, put your picture in the newspapers and what not. Where were you, Aamir?' Dhruv said with a smile, still crying his emotions out.

'I want you to relax now. I want you to believe that we're back!' He said as he sat close to him, Dhruv holding him tight.

'Yes. But did it hurt you very much?'

'That's about right now. Just a little sore here and there. I was scared, but I am much better now. Just some more time and I'll be fit totally.'

'Oh my god, I've missed you so much, Aamir. It's like experiencing a miracle. You've suddenly brought back life into me,' he said, and started coughing while crying.

He knew how difficult his life had been in the last few weeks. 'The feeling is likewise, Dhruv. I too missed you immensely.'

Aamir hugged him some more and tightly this time. In doing that, Dhruv's shirt folded upwards a bit and his stitch marks became visible. Aamir spotted the marks.

'You look quite thin, and what are those stitch marks for?' Aamir said, worried.

'Aamir, it's a very long story. A lot has happened in the last few weeks and it was difficult to absorb.' Dhruv narrated how he had been lucky to save Shantanu's life.

'Dhruv, my god! Are you ok, brother?' This was the side of his brother he never even knew about.

'Yes, I've been in fine form since my operation. Glad to have saved one life and see what god just did to me. He gifted back my own brother.'

'Dhruv, you have done a good deed. I love you for what you've done. You made impossible possible for somebody.'

'Thanks, Aamir. I was always a fool to have ignored you when we were together. It's only after I lost you that I got to know about your importance and followed your path.'

'That sounds sensible. But you were never a fool. I love you for the beautiful person that you are.'

Dhruv turned to Dr. Deshmukh. 'Sir, I haven't had the chance to thank you for what you've been doing for Aamir for the last some weeks since you got him here. But, thank you sir, you've really taken very good care of my brother. You've given your heart and soul to look after him and made it an exceptionally happy moment for both of us. You've been an inspiration. If you wouldn't have found him, we wouldn't have had the chance to be here. It's only because of you that we're here today. You've our hero, sir,' Dhruv said, thankfully. He sat there and closed his eyes, believing that his brother was back and they were together again.

'Don't thank me. I feel wonderful now that I see the two of you back together,' he said. He also reassured them that Aamir was perfectly healthy again and explained how a picture of him and his article got both of them back. His tears were still rolling down his cheeks in happiness. It wasn't hard to figure out that he himself had gotten too attached to Aamir in all these days.

'Please tell me if I can do anything for you. I'll be glad enough to do anything,' Dhruv said.

'I assume that you're like my kids, and whenever I'll need you, you'll be the first ones to hear from me,' he smiled and said.

'Anytime, sir. Thanks again. People like you beat the terror in the world.'

'Enough of praising, Dhruv! This has been a difficult time for all of us. It's time that you guys go back home and spend some quality time with each other. Get some rest.'

He turned to Aamir and said authoritatively, 'You must go and meet Anvi now. She must be expecting you.'

'Yes, sir. I can't wait to see her today.'

After about half an hour, they prepared to leave. Dr. Deshmukh's wife was happy that bringing back Aamir had brought back her husband too. He now had a reason to live, a fresh vigour for life.

Dhruv and Amir were surprised, happy and alive again. These two men couldn't possibly have been happier. They got that lost moment back which they wouldn't give up for anything in the entire world. They talked, laughed and shouted in joy on their way back.

'We've got our whole life to talk about things and laugh. But for now, please take the car to Lilavati Hospital,' Aamir said, worriedly. Dhruv nodded and then, over the next one hour, to the accompaniment of wind and rain outside, told Aamir the things he had done when he hadn't been around. He told Aamir how much he liked Brahmi. By the time he was finished, they reached Lilavati Hospital and Aamir was in a rush to see Anvi.

As soon as he got off his car, Aamir walked as fast as he could towards the hospital room in which Anvi had been placed. Most of the staff recognized him as he had visited Anvi every single day.

A doctor stopped him before he entered Anvi's room. 'Where were you, Aamir? We've been calling you for the last three days and there was no sign of you whatsoever.

Aamir had lost his phone in the terror attack. 'Doctor, I am so sorry. But I am as miserable as you are about this whole situation. I was in the same state as Anvi after the Mumbai local blasts; I was one of the victims.' The doctor's face contorted at the irony. 'I woke up again to recover. But it took me many days. I just came out of the hospital and want to see Anvi. Please allow me.'

'Oh my god! What are you saying, Aamir? I can't even imagine what you've been through. How do you feel now?'

'I am better, but can you please tell me how's Anvi. Am I allowed to meet her please? We'll talk about me later on.'

'Yes sure. Well, Anvi, after all this while has thankfully started regaining consciousness. It's still very early, so she's waking up for just a few minutes daily, and the duration of her being awake should gradually increase with time. This is a very hopeful sign, Aamir. This just happened when we started losing hope,' the doctor said, hopeful and happy. He also made clear that they expected her full recovery in three months if everything stayed positive.

Aamir smiled and thanked the doctor as he thought about his words. He felt his nervousness getting calmed down and excitement going up.

Dhruv had, in the meantime, parked the car outside and joined them. He could see a ray of hope, a better time for him and his family. The rain outside was getting louder as if welcoming all their unexpected happiness. Aamir went into Anvi's room and kissed her forehead as she smiled back for some seconds. Their eyes met before she slept again.

The past month had made Dhruv realize what love and hope is all about. After spending some more time there, they started to go back home. They were both grateful and happy that they had met once again, only to make their brotherhood stronger.

Later that night, the rain had stopped and Aamir had slept after talking for hours with Dhruv and knowing about his whole Brahmi trip. The raindrops remaining on the plant leaves made it a pleasurable scene to watch and Dhruv couldn't help but behold the beauty and believe in this beautiful transition of life he had just experienced. The whole world looked very beautiful, a place which was looking very different the past one month. Tonight, as he thought about his past one month, he felt as if it had changed him a lot as a person, and wondered that following his father's advice of following his intuition and observing everything around had got his lost brother back. He was a survivor, as his father had told him that day and there was certain satisfaction to it.

His thoughts got distracted by a call on his phone. He would never mind answering that call. It was Sachi.

'Hello'

'Hi, Sachi. Good to hear from you.'

'Where the hell have you been, Dhruv? I have been calling you continuously for the last three days and your mobile was always off.'

'It's a long story to tell. So many things have happened in the past few days.'

'You scared me, Dhruv.'

'I am so sorry for that, Sachi.'

'No. I'm sorry, Dhruv.'

'Why are you sorry?'

'For behaving so weird that day in Brahmi. I shouldn't have behaved like that. You were expecting a response from me and I didn't even utter a single word,' she said, unable to hide the guilt in her tone.

'Don't be sorry. I understand how it feels, plus there's something that I wanted to share with you. In fact, a lot of things.'

'Before you say anything, let me surprise you by saying that I'm standing right below your building to meet you. Would you please come down to take a walk here on this beautiful back road?'

'Don't tell me you're serious, Sachi.'

'I am not in a fucking joking mood, Mr. Dhruv. I came all the way to just meet you for some hours and I've my return flight early morning itself,' she said, and she heard the sound of a door opening.

'I'd go back to my flat and jump down if what I am seeing right now is true,' he said happily and hugged Sachi as he reached her.

'Too much? Isn't it?' Sachi gave a shy smile and said.

'No, not at all for the lady who came all the way to Mumbai just to meet me.' He shook his head, his eyes never leaving hers. 'You look beautiful today.' He added.

'Thank you, but you look too lost, tired and thin. See your dark circles too. You promised me and your dad to take care of yourself. Right?' Sachi said, as she pointed out his dark circles.

'Yes, and that's because I had an operation some days back.'

'What? You never told me. You never messaged me to say you're going through an operation, Dhruv.'

As they walked, he turned around to say something, but when he saw her care for him, no words came out of his mouth. All he could do was stare at her. There were suddenly unspoken words hanging in the air between them.

'Would you please tell me what's it regarding?' she said, her voice soft, almost a whisper.

They continued to stare at each other until he finally said something. 'Sachi, after I almost met my dad that day, I felt really privileged to have heard him after long. Which if told to people, they would either make fun of or simply dismiss. But I took every word of what he said very seriously because I had those last hopes of getting Aamir back in my life. I followed my instincts and donated one of my kidneys to somebody close to me, who was in urgent need of it. I believed that if I'd do my part, Aamir somewhere will be proud of that I did something to make a family happier.'

After hearing this, the way she looked at him and felt showed how much she adored him and cared about him. She held his hand to show her support as he finished talking.

'I'm glad you made it happen for somebody, Dhruv. But isn't it in some way going to affect your life?' she asked, cautiously.

'Not at all. People live with one kidney and live all their life normally. Everything has been well taken care of. I just need to be careful of a couple of things and that's it,' he said.

'I am proud of you, Dhruv. You look happier,' she said in response.

Dhruv noticed they were closer together than they had been a month back.

'Yes, I do. But you still don't know the real reason behind it.'

'And what's that?'

'Remember, I just told you over call, I've a lot to tell you.'

'Yes, you did. So tell me.'

He looked at her and smiled, it took her some seconds to register what he wanted to say after looking at the pure happiness in his eyes. She looked at him, moved closer to him, not sure what to say. She hugged him with tears rolling down her eyes for some seconds and after a pause she said, 'Please don't disappoint me by giving any other news now. Please tell me, you got your brother back.'

He looked at her, and while wiping away her tears with his finger, he said, 'You think so?'

'I believe so, Dhruv. You had been looking forward to this day from the day you lost Aamir. You just can't be so happy for any other reason. Your eyes and happiness are saying it all.'

'Sachi, I've missed him all this while. I tried living, but I knew it would never be the same. It's almost like a new birth to me. My father was right about every single word that he said. Just when I came out of the hospital and reached back home, I got to know that a stranger had taken care of my brother all this while after serious injuries and health issues. I donated a life there, and got my brother back here. I wouldn't shout at him anymore, I would listen to him very carefully, take care of him. Not everybody is that lucky to get a lost person back, Sachi. Nothing in the world can trade my feelings right now. I am just too happy today.'

'I am sure, for you never say things that you don't mean. To be honest, I hadn't thought about what surprise I'll get after coming to Mumbai. I think I pretty much liked your surprise here. Probably the best ever surprise.' She said and closed her eyes. 'I missed you so much, Dhruv.'

'I missed you too, Sachi. In fact, I've tried calling you a couple of times and you never responded.'

'Yes, because I knew if I speak to you, I'll break down. And I wanted some time alone to decide my future. I missed you more than anybody else in the last few days. Can you honestly tell me if you still feel the same way about us and will always feel it?'

'Yes,' he said, 'Because I believe that love is much more than just sitting with each other and talking. It's more about how much you miss a person and want to be with him when not around. I was always sure of being with you, but to know that you came all the way just to see me gave me the happiest feeling ever.'

As he said this, he held her in his gaze, and she knew she was in love with him as well. 'Thank you for coming back, Sachi.'

He smiled, waiting for a response, but Sachi seemed content to remain quiet. He held her hand and stood there for some time.

It started raining, and the fact that they were alone and standing hand in hand was a combination of all beautiful things around. It was love. He knew his feelings were real. And so she thought were hers. She knew everything would change if she agrees to it, and she decided to leave the past behind and move on. She allowed herself to give in to her feelings. She knew, agreeing to his proposal would mean sharing a lifetime together and there'd no looking back. But she had never been so sure about spending her whole life with Dhruv. She wanted to imagine everything wonderful and beautiful between them. She had never felt so comfortable in a long time.

They knew they wanted to seize the moment now. It was a beautiful, windy, rainy night and they both were holding each other really tight. It all felt right to her, he felt right. He gently held her hands and in between the hammering rain, they crossed all barriersthat had been stopping them till now. She gave in to her feelings and kissed for the very first time.

Wind and rain joined as one and he could feel her hand tightly holding his. He now ran his hands over her back and kissed her neck. It was not only love, but also holding all the painful memories that they shared. They could feel each other's heart beat. As they became one, the world around them dissolved into something heavenly and magical. This was a moment he wanted neither of them to forget.

At last, love, hope, humanity and belief had won…together. Could there be any better end to this day?

Epilogue

My belief in miracles became stronger in that last magical month when I first lost and then found Aamir. I followed everything you said very carefully, Dad. Our story will never really end as it has secured a place in everybody's heart.

I cannot help but be moved when I think of the struggle you undertook to give both of us this beautiful life. Because of you, I have the strength to go on with my life. I am no longer afraid. Life is bigger than any of us. We no longer feel alone and distressed. We know you are watching over us. You are never going to leave us. I have stopped over-thinking and I just let things happen and run their course.

You always knew how to make me feel good within. I know that somehow, every step I took after I returned from Brahmi was a step to find Aamir. The Dhruv who returned from that journey was not the same man. I believe in wonders, magic, miracles. These take place every day, no matter how inexplicable or unbelievable. We just need to keep our hearts and eyes open to see them.

Now, standing in the balcony of our very own home in Mumbai with Aamir, I know this is the best thing that could happen to me after those terrorist attacks. Had it not been for you, I would never have had this opportunity to meet Aamir again. I have finally understood that there are far better things ahead in the future than any we leave behind in the past. The only way to discover if something better is waiting for us is to first believe that there is something better out there. I do believe now.

Finally, I am in the room where I shared most of our life. This flat is special for me; that's why I bought it to relive my memories of our lives together. I sit and look around the kitchen again, where Aamir fed me morning, evening and night, even when I returned home heavily drunk. I know his surely is the love that is greater than anybody else's on earth. And in an odd way, I have come to believe that I'd learned more in those few days than I had in all the years before or after.

I now understand the difficulties Aamir endured to raise me and I realize how painful it must have been for him to move on after you and mother. Although I understand that we will never see each other again, Dad, I wonder if there's a way to see you and give you a hug once more in this life. I also try to remember the way we once were, what we used to do during the holidays and all the fun we had.

Anvi is totally fine now. Six months after the incident, Anvi and Aamir got married after venturing too far into a beautiful and honest relationship. We're a happy family now. I took a family picture and sat looking through it and made myself believe that we're together. My joy and sense of belonging to them is something more special than anything else in the world. As a gift to them, I decided to write a story based on Aamir's and Anvi's relationship and get the novel published. When I approached the publishers with the manuscript after some months of my finishing it, their responses were overwhelming. I wasn't able to believe it for some days. *I Still Think About You* is up on everybody's heart, everywhere and people's love for Aamir and Anvi has made a special place in millions of hearts by now.

With time, I too realized what I am good at. So, I am working as a columnist for a leading Indian newspaper and also looking out for one more real stories like that of Aamir and Anvi which can re-define love. It's beautiful to see people appreciating me and my work. And you'd be happy to know that I've got a new family too, Mithun's family. They take very good care of me and make sure that we meet quite often.

I am going to go on yet another journey to Brahmi with Sachi. With time, we realized that it was your blessings that made us fall in love with each other. There's no moment less special with her. Maybe I'll hear your voice again. We need your blessings. And maybe, I'll relive those moments again, Dad. I hope to see you there once again in the middle of heaven, this time with Mom. Be with me always. Take any form, guide me through.

Brahmi indeed holds me on, still; and always will.